*Everyman, I will go with thee,
and be thy guide*

THE EVERYMAN
LIBRARY

*The Everyman Library was founded by J. M. Dent
in 1906. He chose the name Everyman because he wanted
to make available the best books ever written in every
field to the greatest number of people at the cheapest possible
price. He began with Boswell's 'Life of Johnson';
his one-thousandth title was Aristotle's 'Metaphysics',
by which time sales exceeded forty million.*

*Today Everyman paperbacks remain true to
J. M. Dent's aims and high standards, with a wide range
of titles at affordable prices in editions which address
the needs of today's readers. Each new text is reset to give
a clear, elegant page and to incorporate the latest thinking
and scholarship. Each book carries the pilgrim logo,
the character in 'Everyman', a medieval morality play,
a proud link between Everyman
past and present.*

Joseph Conrad

THE HEART OF DARKNESS

Edited by
CEDRIC WATTS
University of Sussex

EVERYMAN
J. M. DENT · LONDON
CHARLES E. TUTTLE
VERMONT

Introduction and other editorial material
© Cedric Watts 1995

Heart of Darkness first published in Everyman 1967
This 1899 edition of *The Heart of Darkness*
first published in Everyman in 1995
Reprinted with revisions 1996

15 17 19 20 18 16 14

J. M. Dent
Orion Publishing Group,
Orion House,
5 Upper St Martin's Lane,
London WC2H 9EA
and
Tuttle Publishing,
Airport Industrial Park,
364 Innovation Drive,
North Clarendon,
VT 05759-9436,
USA

Typeset in Sabon by Deltatype Ltd, Ellesmere Port, Cheshire
Printed in Great Britain by
Clays Ltd, St Ives plc

British Library Cataloguing-in-Publication Data
is available upon request.

ISBN 978-0-4608-7477-9

The Orion Publishing Group's policy is to use papers that
are natural, renewable and recyclable products and
made from wood grown in sustainable forests. The logging
and manufacturing processes are expected to conform to
the environmental regulations of the country of origin.

www.orionbooks.co.uk

CONTENTS

NOTE ON THE AUTHOR AND EDITOR

JOSEPH CONRAD (originally Jósef Teodor Konrad Nałęcz Korzeniowski) was born in the Russian-dominated area of Poland in 1857. His parents were punished by the Russians for their Polish nationalist activities, and both died while Conrad was still a child. In 1874 he left Poland for France, where he began his maritime career. He attempted suicide in 1878 but survived to join the British Merchant Navy, and completed nearly twenty years at sea before becoming a full-time novelist. He took British nationality in 1886 and settled permanently in England in the 1890s, marrying Jessie George in 1896.

Almayer's Folly, Conrad's first novel, appeared in 1895. His major texts, which include 'Heart of Darkness', *Lord Jim, Nostromo, The Secret Agent* and *Under Western Eyes*, are characterised by descriptive richness and eloquence, narrative obliquity, searching scepticism and sustained irony: dramatic plots undergo sophisticated mutation. Though his works were often highly acclaimed, sales were disappointing until, in 1914, the commercial success of *Chance* brought Conrad financial security and general fame; eventually he was offered a knighthood, which he declined. He died in 1924. Conrad's writings have exerted a powerful cultural influence which may be discerned in the works of (for example) T. S. Eliot, Scott Fitzgerald, Graham Greene, Orson Welles, Ngugi wa Thiong'o and Howard Brenton. He is widely regarded as one of the greatest fiction-writers in English, though in recent years his standing has become a matter of critical contention.

CEDRIC WATTS is Professor of English at the University of Sussex. His numerous books on Conrad include *The Deceptive Text* (1984), *Joseph Conrad: A Literary Life* (1989) and *A Preface to Conrad* (2nd edn, 1993). *A Preface to Greene* appeared in 1997, and *Henry V, War Criminal?* in 2000.

CHRONOLOGY OF CONRAD'S LIFE

Year	Age	Life
1857		Józef Teodor Konrad Nałęcz Korzeniowski (Joseph Conrad) born in the Ukraine on 3 December
1861	3	Conrad's father, Apollo Korzeniowski, arrested in Warsaw for patriotic conspiracy
1862	4	Conrad's parents exiled to Vologda, Russia; he goes with them
1863	5	Family moves to Chernikhov
1865	7	Death of Conrad's mother, Ewelina Korzeniowska
1869	11	Death of his father. Tadeusz Bobrowski becomes his guardian
1870	12	Taught by Adam Pulman in Kraków
1871	13	Also taught by Izydor Kopernicki
1872	14	Resolves to go to sea
1873	15	Tour of Switzerland with Adam Pulman
1874	16	Leaves Poland for Marseille
1875	17	Sails Atlantic in *Mont-Blanc*
1876	18	Serves as steward in *Saint-Antoine*
1878	20	Shoots himself, recovers, and joins British ship *Mavis*
1879	21	Serves in clipper *Duke of Sutherland*
1880	22	Sails to Australia in *Loch Etive*
1881	23	Second mate of *Palestine*

CHRONOLOGY OF HIS TIMES

Year	Literary Context	Historical Events
1857	Flaubert, *Madame Bovary*	Indian Mutiny begins
	Baudelaire, *Les Fleurs du mal*	
1859	Dickens, *A Tale of Two Cities*	Darwin, *Origin of Species*
1861	Dickens, *Great Expectations*	American Civil War begins
	George Eliot, *Silas Marner*	Nansen born
1862	Turgenev, *Fathers and Sons*	Bismarck gains power in
	Hugo, *Les Misérables*	Prussia
1863	Thackeray dies	American slaves freed
		Polish uprising
1865	Kipling and Yeats born	American Civil War ends
1869	Tolstoy, *War and Peace*	Gandhi born
	Gide born	Suez Canal opens
1870	Dickens dies	Franco-Prussian War
1871	Dostoyevsky, *The Devils*	Paris Commune
1872	George Eliot, *Middlemarch*	Mazzini dies
	Butler, *Erewhon*	Bertrand Russell born
1873	Ford Madox Hueffer born	Livingstone dies
1874	Hardy, *Far From the Madding Crowd*	Churchill born
1875	Mann born	Schweitzer born
1876	George Sand dies	Queen Victoria declared
	James, *Roderick Hudson*	Empress of India
1878	Hardy, *The Return of the Native*	Second Afghan War
		Congress of Berlin
1879	Ibsen, *A Doll's House*	Zulu War
	Meredith, *The Egoist*	Einstein and Stalin born
1880	Dostoyevsky, *The Brothers Karamazov*	Boer uprising in Transvaal
1881	Dostoyevsky and Carlyle die	Tsar Alexander II assassinated

Year	Age	Life
1882	24	Storm-damaged *Palestine* repaired
1883	25	Shipwrecked when *Palestine* sinks
1885	27	Sails to Calcutta in *Tilkhurst*
1886	28	Becomes a British subject; qualifies as captain
1887	29	Sails to Java in *Highland Forest*
1888	30	Master of the *Otago*, his sole command
1889	31	Resigns from *Otago*; begins to write *Almayer's Folly*
1890	32	Works in Congo Free State
1891	33	Mate of *Torrens* (until 1893)
1892	34	Voyages to Australia
1893	35–6	Visits Bobrowski in Ukraine. Joins steamship *Adowa*
1894	36	*Almayer's Folly* accepted by Unwin. Meets Edward Garnett and Jessie George
1895	37	*Almayer's Folly* published. Completes *An Outcast of the Islands*
1896	38	*An Outcast of the Islands* published. Marries Jessie George
1897	39	Befriended by Cunninghame Graham. *The Nigger of the 'Narcissus'*
1898	40	First son (Borys) born. *Tales of Unrest*. Collaborates with Ford Madox Hueffer (later surnamed Ford). Friendship with Stephen Crane
1899	41	'The Heart of Darkness' serialised. Serialisation of *Lord Jim* begins
1900	42	*Lord Jim* (book). J. B. Pinker becomes Conrad's agent
1901	43	*The Inheritors* (co-author Hueffer)
1902	44	*Youth* volume (including 'Heart of Darkness')
1903	45	*Typhoon* volume. *Romance* (co-author Hueffer)
1904	46	*Nostromo*
1905	47	*One Day More* (play) fails

Year	Literary Context	Historical Events
1882	Virginia Woolf and Joyce born	Darwin and Garibaldi die
1883	Nietzsche, *Thus Spake Zarathustra*	Marx dies Mussolini born
1885	D. H. Lawrence born	'Congo Free State' recognised
1886	Stevenson, *Dr Jekyll and Mr Hyde*	Salisbury becomes premier Graham becomes MP
1887	Marianne Moore born	'Bloody Sunday' riot in London
1888	T. S. Eliot born	Wilhelm II becomes Kaiser
1889	Browning dies	Hitler born
1890	Ibsen, *Hedda Gabler*	Bismarck resigns
1891	Hardy, *Tess of the d'Urbervilles*	Parnell dies
1892	Tennyson dies	Gladstone's fourth ministry
1893	Maupassant dies	Independent Labour Party formed
1894	Stevenson dies Huxley born	Nicholas II becomes Tsar Greenwich explosion
1895	Crane, *The Red Badge of Courage*	Marconi invents 'wireless' telegraphy
1896	Morris and Verlaine die Chekhov, *The Seagull*	Nobel Prizes established
1897	Kipling, *Captains Courageous* James, *What Maisie Knew*	Queen Victoria's Diamond Jubilee
1898	Wilde, 'The Ballad of Reading Gaol' Wells, *The War of the Worlds*	War between Spain and USA Bismarck and Gladstone die Fashoda incident
1899	Hemingway born	Dreyfus freed Boer War begins
1900	Ruskin, Wilde and Crane die	Russia occupies Manchuria
1901	Kipling, *Kim*	Queen Victoria dies
1902	Zola dies	Boer War ends
1903	James, *The Ambassadors*	First powered aircraft flight
1904	Chekhov, *The Cherry Orchard*	Russo-Japanese War begins
1905	Wells, *Kipps*	Russia defeated by Japan

Year	Age	Life
1906	48	Second son (John) born. *The Mirror of the Sea* (aided by Hueffer)
1907	49	*The Secret Agent*
1908	50	*A Set of Six* (tales). Heavily indebted to Pinker. Involved in *English Review*
1909	51	Quarrels with Hueffer
1910	52	Nervous breakdown on completion of *Under Western Eyes*. Awarded a Civil List pension of £100 per year
1911	53	*Under Western Eyes* published
1912	54	*Some Reminiscences* (later known by the title of the USA edition, *A Personal Record*). *'Twixt Land and Sea* (tales). *Chance* serialised in *New York Herald*
1913	55	Meets Bertrand Russell
1914	56	Book of *Chance* has large sales. Conrad prospers
1915	57	*Within the Tides* (tales). *Victory*. Borys Conrad enlists in Army
1916	58	Conrad flies in a naval aircraft and goes to sea in H.M.S. *Ready*
1917	59	*The Shadow-Line*. Conrad in poor health. Relinquishes Civil List pension
1918	60	Borys Conrad wounded in war. *Typhon* (Gide's translation of *Typhoon*)
1919	61	*The Arrow of Gold*. Macdonald Hastings' version of *Victory* staged. Film of *Victory*
1920	62	*The Rescue* (published 24 years after commencement). Conrad and Pinker adapt 'Gaspar Ruiz'
1920–8		Collected editions by Doubleday (N.Y.), Heinemann (London), Gresham (London) and Grant (Edinburgh)
1921	63	*Notes on Life and Letters*
1922	64	Death of Pinker. Conrad meets Ravel. Borys marries. *The Secret Agent* (play) fails

Year	Literary Context	Historical Events
1906	Beckett born Ibsen dies	Liberals win British election
1907	Auden born	Lord Kelvin dies
1908	Bennett, *The Old Wives' Tale* Forster, *A Room with a View*	Feminist agitation; Mrs Pankhurst jailed
1909	Swinburne dies	Blériot flies across Channel
1910	Forster, *Howards End* Yeats, *The Green Helmet*	King Edward VII dies; accession of George V
1911	Golding born	Industrial unrest in UK
1912	Patrick White born Pound, *Ripostes*	First Balkan War Sinking of *Titanic* Wilson elected President
1913	Lawrence, *Sons and Lovers*	Second Balkan War
1914	Joyce, *Dubliners*	World War I begins
1915	Lawrence's *The Rainbow* banned	Italy enters war Gallipoli disaster
1916	James dies Joyce, *A Portrait*	Battle of Jutland Battle of the Somme
1917	T. S. Eliot, *Prufrock* Anthony Burgess born	USA enters war Russian Revolution
1918	Rosenberg and Owen die Wyndham Lewis, *Tarr*	Armistice Polish Republic restored Women enfranchised in UK
1919	Virginia Woolf, *Night and Day* Hardy, *Poetical Works*	UK's first woman MP Versailles Treaty
1920	Lawrence, *Women in Love* Katherine Mansfield, *Bliss*	Poles rout Russian invaders League of Nations created
1921	Huxley, *Crome Yellow*	Irish Free State founded
1922	T. S. Eliot, *The Waste Land* Joyce, *Ulysses*	Mussolini gains power in Italy

Year	Age	Life
1923	65	Declines honorary degree from Cambridge. Acclaimed on visit to USA. *The Rover*
1923–7		Collected ('Uniform') edition by Dent (London)
1924	66	Declines knighthood. Dies of heart attack; buried at Canterbury
1925		*Tales of Hearsay* and the incomplete *Suspense*
1926		*Last Essays*
1927		*Joseph Conrad: Life & Letters*, written and edited by G. Jean-Aubry

Year	Literary Context	Historical Events
1923	Yeats wins Nobel Prize Wells, *Men Like Gods*	Moscow becomes capital of USSR
1924	Forster, *A Passage to India* Shaw, *St Joan* Anatole France dies	Lenin dies MacDonald heads first Labour Government in UK
1925	T. S. Eliot, *Poems 1909–25*	Hitler publishes *Mein Kampf*
1926	Kafka, *The Castle*	General Strike in UK
1927	Virginia Woolf, *To the* *Lighthouse*	Lindbergh flies Atlantic

INTRODUCTION

In the century after its first appearance, the fame and influence of 'Heart of Darkness' have become so great that even people who have never read the text are encountering it obliquely – in films, poems and novels influenced by it, in journalistic references, in passing allusions. It is Conrad's most intense, subtle, compressed, profound and proleptic work: proleptic because it anticipated so many later cultural developments. It is a work of genius which has unfolded its many meanings as the decades have advanced.

By the 1970s, 'Heart of Darkness' was acclaimed by many critics as a supreme literary achievement. To C. B. Cox, it was 'one of those amazing modern fictions . . . . . which throw light on the whole nature of modern art'; for Lionel Trilling, it contained 'in sum the whole of the radical critique of European civilization that has been made by literature in the years since its publication.'[1] In the final quarter of the twentieth century, however, the tale has come under attack from various directions. Marxists and post-colonial writers have argued that it is deeply implicated in imperialism and is racist; feminists have alleged that it is imperialist, racist and sexist. Once seen as radical, liberating, challenging and subversive, 'Heart of Darkness' is now seen by a range of commentators as 'politically incorrect'. And this highly ironic tale continues to generate ironies. By its bold originality it helped to bring about the very changes which, eventually, facilitated adverse criticisms. A tale about ambushes, it can still ambush its commentators; a sceptical work, it can still mock the prejudices of its critics. Above all, by its combinations of intellectual subtlety and satiric boldness, of linguistic verve and graphic vividness, it still exposes by contrast the thin texture and limited range of so much critical and political discourse.

*

To judge the tale fairly, and to appreciate its originality, we need to remember that Joseph Conrad wrote it in 1898–9 and that it was first published (as 'The Heart of Darkness' – its 'The' was dropped later) early in 1899. Hence the text used for this edition. Other extant editions of the tale are based on later copy-texts. The first version, however, published in *Blackwood's Magazine* between February and April, 1899, is more radical than those later versions, more so even than the 1902 text incorporated in the book, *Youth: A Narrative / and / Two Other Stories*. It is more radical not because of differences in content (though there *are* some significant differences, as the 'Note on the Text' will show) but because of the difference in context. For instance, the serial version appeared before the Boer War, whereas the book appeared after it; the serial appeared in the Victorian age, the book in the Edwardian age. If it is regarded as an early twentieth-century text, its techniques and insights are remarkable enough; if it is regarded as a late nineteenth-century text, they are phenomenal.

The tale's linguistic verve is the more striking when we recall that Conrad was writing in a foreign language. He was Polish by birth, and spent many years at sea; he had not studied at university. A person writing a tale in a foreign language might well be inclined to play safe, aiming to avoid errors, taking no stylistic risks. Conrad, writing in the language of his adoptive country, took astonishing risks in his fiction. In 'The Heart of Darkness', for example, the styles employed include: the colloquially conversational and idiomatic; the philosophically sophisticated; the impressionistically descriptive; the poetically lyrical; the satiric, the ironic, the laconic. Its modes blend realism with symbolism. Conrad rejoices in ambiguity and the paradoxical. Indeed, it looks as though what might have been a liability became a remarkable asset: precisely because he was writing in a foreign language, Conrad was particularly aware of the ways in which language may deceive and delude, particularly conscious of the disparities between fact and phrase, deed and declamation, reality and propaganda. So one of the many paradoxes of 'The Heart of

Darkness' is that it offers eloquent criticisms of eloquence; with immense linguistic virtuosity, it lets scepticism play upon credulity about language's relationship to reality.

A related paradox is that while making a number of traditional moral affirmations (for the tale affirms, through Marlow, the value of courage, kindness and honesty), it directs a penetrating scepticism at the notion that morality has some absolute basis. Life, we are told, is 'that mysterious arrangement of merciless logic for a futile purpose'. Repeatedly Marlow, the tale's principal narrator, suggests that civilised morality is a matter of conventions sustained by 'the butcher and the policeman', and that once a person is taken away from society's customary supports, almost any change, any descent into corruption or barbarism, becomes a possibility. To us, now, such scepticism may seem familiar; in 1899, in a work of literature, it was altogether bolder. And it is typical of the complexity of 'The Heart of Darkness' that it can be sceptical even about scepticism. Though Marlow seems generally atheistic, he invokes the supernatural. The tale takes on a 'Gothic' quality when Kurtz's corruption is being described; and part of that Gothic effect derives from the hints that Kurtz participates in metaphysical evil; there is something Satanic and vampiric about the forces that tempt him.[2] Yet, in the extremity of his corruption he is both contemptible and awe-inspiring: there are even suggestions that he has gained a stature, a significance, denied to average humdrum people. And he inspires loyalty, not least in the Africans among whom he lives.

If it is borne in mind that the tale appeared in 1899, in the reign of Queen Victoria, one of its most striking features appears to be its satiric indictment of the rapacity, cruelty and folly of the European traders in central Africa. At that time, a majority of its readers would almost certainly have been enthusiastic about imperialism. This was the heyday of empires; the great powers were competing for raw materials, territory and markets abroad. In 1876 Queen Victoria had been proclaimed Empress of India; and, in 1897, the celebrations at her Diamond Jubilee were seen as a glorification of the British Empire. A commentator remarked at the time:

> We are Imperialists first, and Liberals or Tories afterwards. I said
> this, for my own part, years ago, when the sentiment was not quite
> so popular. Now it has happily become a commonplace. The
> Jubilee is its culminating expression . . . . .[3]

In extent of land and size of population, the British Empire was
the greatest the world had known, embracing (among other
regions) Canada, Australia, New Zealand, India (including
Pakistan and Burma), British Guiana, parts of the East Indies and
Antarctica, and large tracts of Africa. In the last twenty years of
the century, rivalry between the great powers accelerated. The
United States emerged as a new imperialist power, successfully
warring against Spain and securing Cuba. Germany embarked on
an armaments race with Great Britain which was to have its fatal
culmination in the 1914–18 War.

In addition to Britain, numerous European nations sought to
colonise and exploit Africa: Dutch settlers (the Boers) had long
occupied much of the south; the French controlled much of the
north and centre; and Germany, Portugal, Spain and Belgium had
claimed large tracts. In 1885 the Sudanese had rebelled against the
British authorities, defeating General Gordon's troops; Gordon
himself was killed. But in September 1898 Gordon's death was
bloodily avenged: General Kitchener's forces vanquished the
Sudanese; general jubilation followed in the British press. Next, in
the 'Fashoda Incident', the British prevented the French from
linking their African territories from west to east. Then, several
months after the publication of 'The Heart of Darkness', the Boer
War began in South Africa. The Boers in the Transvaal and the
Orange Free State had resented the influx of British prospectors
from the Cape of Good Hope, a British colony, and formed a
military alliance. The British sent troops; the Boer states declared
war. After many early victories, the Boers were defeated in 1902,
and were obliged to accept British sovereignty. Again, in England
that war – which Conrad deemed 'idiotic'[4] – occasioned intense
patriotic and imperialistic fervour. English fiction of that era
tended to reflect and endorse imperialistic sentiments. Of novels
dealing with Africa, one of the most popular for many years was
Henry Rider Haggard's *King Solomon's Mines* (1885), in which

three intrepid British explorers succeed not only in securing a fortune in diamonds but also in overthrowing a tribal tyrant and installing an indigenous ruler whom they have taught the principles of just government. The whites have demonstrated their valour and resourcefulness, advanced the cause of civilisation, and made themselves rich.

The region described in 'The Heart of Darkness' is not named (for good reason, to generalise the narrative's implications), but it corresponds more closely to the Congo Free State than to any other part of Africa. The adjective 'Free' in that title proved to be hypocritical. Advocates of imperialism in Africa advanced a wide range of justifications for their activities. Sometimes the justification was 'destiny': imperial action seemed to be a mystically-fated or divinely-ordained necessity. (Rudyard Kipling's poems amplified this view.) Sometimes it was the noble culmination of the 'work ethic': Thomas Carlyle had called on the 'Workers' (with a capital W) to convert the darkness of 'savagery and despair' into 'a kind of heaven' – 'It is work for a God'.[5] A related justification was 'historical necessity', which appealed to Darwinian notions of the struggle for survival. Lord Salisbury, the Conservative Prime Minister, declared in May 1898 (to appreciative laughter from his audience at the Albert Hall, and to private scorn from Conrad):

> From the necessities of politics or under the pretence of philanthropy – the living nations will gradually encroach on the territory of the dying . . . It is not to be supposed that any one nation of the living nations will be allowed to have the profitable monopoly of curing or cutting up these unfortunate patients . . . . .[6]

And commonly, of course, the justification was one of those which Lord Salisbury had termed 'the pretence of philanthropy': it was the evident duty of the civilised nations to confer the benefits of civilisation (Christianity, education, law and order, trade) on those benighted heathen with their barbaric ways. In the Congo, that hypocrisy reached its extremity; and Conrad, looking back, saw there 'the vilest scramble for loot that ever disfigured the history of human conscience'.[7] Generally he scorned those conventional, 'politically correct', doctrines of his day. His essay 'Autocracy and War' treats all imperialism as a destructive folly born of greed, ignorance and moral immaturity.[8]

In 1890, when Conrad travelled there, the 'Congo Free State' ('L'Etat Indépendant du Congo') was the private property of King Leopold II of Belgium. Leopold's declared aim was:

> to open to civilisation the only part of our globe where Christianity has not penetrated and to pierce the darkness which envelops the entire population.

His agents there, he said,

> have always present in their minds a strong sense of the career of honour in which they are engaged, and are animated with a pure feeling of patriotism; not sparing their own blood, they will the more spare the blood of the natives, who will see in them the all-powerful protectors of their lives and of their property, benevolent teachers of whom they have so great a need.[9]

The disparity between such words and the reality was extreme. Leopold's claim to the region was of dubious legality; and the Belgian activities in the Congo were almost wholly exploitative. The main aim was to extract as much ivory and rubber from the area as possible; Africans were virtually enslaved for the purpose, maltreated and mutilated, coerced and starved. Gradually these facts became publicised, and an international outcry was heard. Roger Casement, whom Conrad had met in the Congo, and to whom the author sent encouraging letters,[10] published in 1904 a damning report for the British parliament. Casement had read and praised 'Heart of Darkness', and consulted Conrad during preparation of his report. After its publication, the Congo Reform Association was founded by E. D. Morel to protest against Leopold's exploitation of the Africans. Via Casement, Conrad supplied to Morel, for his campaign, a statement condemning the Belgian régime in the Congo. It said, for instance:

> It is an extraordinary thing that the conscience of Europe which seventy years ago has put down the slave trade on humanitarian grounds tolerates the Congo State to day. It is as if the moral clock

had been put back many hours . . . . . [T]here exists in Africa a Congo State . . . where ruthless, systematic cruelty towards the blacks is the basis of administration . . . . .[11]

This statement was quoted at length in Morel's book, *King Leopold's Rule in Africa* (1904); and the London *Morning Post*, in a laudatory review, gave particular prominence to Conrad's 'heavy indictment'.[12] In a letter to Sir Arthur Conan Doyle, Morel later remarked that 'Heart of Darkness' was 'the most powerful thing ever written on the subject'.[13] Undoubtedly the campaign helped to bring about reforms which mitigated the harshness of the colonial régime. The campaigners' goal of seeing administration transferred from Leopold to the Belgian parliament was achieved in 1908.[14] A judicious analyst of these matters has concluded:

We cannot know how many people Conrad's Congo fiction informed and moved to indignation, but we at least know that, despite its overshadowing darkness, Conrad's work provided solid inspiration to the reformers.[15]

Conrad's linguistic scepticism had made him particularly sensitive to the disparity between imperial rhetoric and exploitative actuality. There was another and more obvious reason for his critical awareness. Conrad's own family were victims of imperialism. He had been born into a Poland which had vanished from the map of Europe after a series of 'partitions' which divided Poland between Prussia, Austria and Russia. Conrad was brought up in the Russian-dominated area; his parents, loyal patriots, conspired against the oppressive authorities, and were sentenced to exile; as a child, Conrad accompanied them on the bleak journey to Vologda. It is not surprising, then, that when he travelled in central Africa in 1890, hoping to command a steamboat on the Congo river, he should have been alert to the ways in which the Africans were suffering under imposed rule. Sometimes, in the tale, the attitude to the indigenous people is condescending or apprehensive; Marlow uses the term 'nigger' with the casual insouciance which was common at that period;[16] but again and again the tale voices indignation at the barbarities inflicted on the Africans in the name of 'progress' and 'civilisation'.

In Marlow's narrative, ironic and graphic juxtapositions repeatedly make the point. The only vital and joyous people in the tale are a group of as-yet-uncolonised Africans who are seen paddling their canoe through the surf:

> They shouted, sang; their bodies streamed with perspiration; they had faces like grotesque masks – these chaps; but they had bone, muscle, a wild vitality, an intense energy of movement, that was as natural and true as the surf along their coast. They wanted no excuse for being there.[17]

'They wanted no excuse': it is their homeland; unlike the European invaders, they are exuberantly alive in the environment. In direct contrast to that canoe is the French warship which, absurdly, is shelling the African continent:

> In the empty immensity of earth, sky, and water, there she was, incomprehensible, firing into a continent. Pop, would go one of the eight-inch guns; a small flame would dart and vanish, a little white smoke would disappear, a tiny projectile would give a feeble screech – and nothing happened. Nothing could happen. There was a touch of insanity in the proceeding, a sense of lugubrious drollery in the sight; and it was not dissipated by somebody on board assuring me earnestly there was a camp of natives – he called them enemies! – hidden out of sight somewhere.[18]

Repeatedly the tale illustrates the 'touch of insanity' in colonialism: the incongruity, absurdity and destructive folly. (Indeed, with satirist's licence, Conrad exaggerates its incompetence.) At the outer station, the whites are, officially, 'building a railway'; what Marlow sees is a chaos of decaying machinery, rusting rails and 'objectless blasting'. The labourers are the chained and starving slaves:

> They walked erect and slow, balancing small baskets full of earth on their heads, and the clink kept time with their footsteps. Black rags were wound round their loins, and the short ends behind wagged to and fro like tails. I could see every rib, the joints of their limbs were like knots in a rope; each had an iron collar on his neck, and all were connected together with a chain whose bights swung between them, rhythmically clinking. Another report from the cliff

made me think suddenly of that ship of war I had seen firing into a continent. It was the same kind of ominous voice; but these men could by no stretch of imagination be called enemies. They were called criminals, and the outraged law, like the bursting shells, had come to them, an insoluble mystery from over the sea. All their meagre breasts panted together, the violently dilated nostrils quivered, the eyes stared stonily up-hill.[19]

Repeatedly, such visually-sharp descriptions drive a wedge between the philanthropic rhetoric of the colonisers and the harsh reality. Leopold claimed to be eradicating slavery from central Africa; the tale depicts the new slavery that the colonists created. Instead of so-called 'enemies' or 'criminals', the narrative depicts suffering African people. Whether the familiar clichés be those of conventional law and order, of progress and efficiency, or even (eventually) of idealistic love, the narrative undercuts them. 'Rebels' is the term for the sacrificial victims whose skulls grace Kurtz's compound; Kurtz's humanitarian rhetoric is mocked by his descent into corruption and by his exclamation, 'Exterminate all the brutes!'; to the company's manager, 'unsound method' sums up the corrupt rapacity that Kurtz has displayed; and eventually the romantic clichés used by Kurtz's fiancée are mocked by their object, the depraved Kurtz himself.

One point made by the depiction of Kurtz is that the defilement of Africa may result from the activities not only of mercenary exploiters like the manager and his uncle but also of ambitious idealists. Conrad has striven to make Kurtz a representative figure: 'All Europe contributed to the making of Kurtz'; 'his mother was half-English, his father was half-French'; he 'had been educated partly in England'. So, whereas the opening of the tale (particularly Marlow's reference to the red parts of the map of the world, those British territories where 'some real work is done') might encourage the reader to assume that British people are aloof from the corruption depicted, the narrative involves England in the exploitation. Even the little detail of the 'bones', the ivory dominoes used by the accountant who listens to Marlow's tale, suggests a degree of complicity with the brutal ivory-trade the tale depicts.

Near the beginning of his narrative, Marlow casts about, trying to define some feature which might redeem imperialism: 'efficiency', perhaps, or 'an idea', or 'an unselfish belief in the idea'; later he proffers 'restraint' and 'principles'. Gradually, his story shows the inadequacies of each of these factors. The ruthless accountant at the central station is an efficient book-keeper; Kurtz was sincerely idealistic; the cannibal crew displays restraint (indeed, it is apparently Kurtz rather than the crew who eats human flesh); and Marlow observes that 'superstitions, beliefs, and what you may call principles, . . . are less than chaff in a breeze', when confronted with hunger. By the end of the tale practically every justification has been eroded; the dominant impression is of 'robbery with violence, aggravated murder on a great scale, and men going at it blind'. One is left with the shrewdly sceptical definition of a majestic phrase:

> The conquest of the earth . . . . . mostly means the taking it away from those who have a different complexion or slightly flatter noses than ourselves . . . . .[20]

Thus, modern imperialism proves no better than the ancient Roman version, which Marlow had initially portrayed as inferior; his 'young citizen in a toga' is an ancestor of Kurtz. One of Conrad's methods in the tale is to establish contrasts which are then eroded. The very title, 'The Heart of Darkness', invites the reader to think of 'the heart of darkest Africa'; but the contrast between the primitive and the civilised is eroded first by the suggestions that London itself may be a centre of brooding gloom, and secondly by the recognition of the moral darkness within Kurtz. Initially, Kurtz seems to offer a promising contrast to the mercenary pilgrims; but he proves to be depraved, and the contrast which then emerges is that between his intensity of corruption and their automatic avarice. His fiancée, nobly statuesque in the darkening drawing room of the 'sepulchral city', seems to contrast with Kurtz's African consort; but the latter, too, is nobly statuesque; she too, has charms (literal as well as metaphorical); she, too, is devoted to the charismatic leader, to the genius who, in Europe, might have become a leading politician; and both women are termed 'tragic'. Thus the tale's ironies challenge not only imperial hubris but also the pride and presumption of civilisation itself. Marlow on his return to Europe (rather like Swift's returning Gulliver) feels like laughing scornfully in the faces of the unwitting people in the streets.

*

Conrad was a pioneer of the literary modernism which burgeoned in the early twentieth century, reaching its peak around 1922 (when Eliot's *The Waste Land*, Joyce's *Ulysses* and Woolf's *Jacob's Room* appeared). Modernist literature often effected ironic juxtapositions of the ancient and the modern; it emphasised subjectivity and relativism of perception; it suggested that the present was a time of crisis in which old certitudes were crumbling; significance itself became problematic. Favoured techniques included ironic obliquity, symbolic density and allusions to myth. These features were already present in 'The Heart of Darkness'.

The allusions by Marlow to Roman civilisation, particularly to that time when Britain might have seemed a benighted wilderness to the Roman adventurer, serve to suggest the cycles of imperial domination, a repeated historic process of emergence and recession. Marlow's keenly self-aware narrative, with its emphasis on his isolation from the other travellers (and on general human isolation: 'We live, as we dream – alone'); his sense of absurdity, and his doubt about communicating the significant to his hearers: these features and themes were to resonate in so much literature of the subsequent fifty years. 'Kafkaesque' effects proleptically abound in the tale: in the depiction of the company's urban headquarters, where the organisation is sinister, fatal and inscrutable; in the obscurely conspiratorial conversations; in the nightmarish and black-comic features of the journey. T. S. Eliot and Graham Greene (both admirers of 'Heart of Darkness')[21] amplified the appalling paradox that secular existence may lack significance, whereas evil confers intensity. The suggestion that civilisation is only skin deep, and may conceal either vacuity or a potential for brutality, would be developed by many writers, among them André Gide and Thomas Mann. Both Freudian and Jungian concepts had been anticipated by the tale: Freudian, in the rendering of Kurtz's depravity; Jungian, in evoking a perilous journey into the self which is also a descent into the mythical past.

In some respects, in the depictions of radical absurdity, of a quest for authenticity, and of the defiance of bourgeois conventions, 'The Heart of Darkness' foreshadowed the existentialist writings of Sartre and Camus which became fashionable around fifty years later. Historical crises in the twentieth century conferred a prophetic quality on the narrative; the slaughter of the Great War and the horrors of Nazism seemed to validate much of its pessimism; George Steiner's *The Portage to San Cristobal of A. H.* fused Kurtz and Hitler; and in 1979, in the film *Apocalypse Now*, the tale was blended with the destructive absurdities and confusions of the Vietnamese War.

'Heart of Darkness' thus proved to possess a remarkable epitomising quality. Whether by its epigrammatic phrasing, its vivid cameos, or its ironic narrative structures, it provided epitomic anticipations of, and critical commentaries on, cultural and historical events to come. Since it was at once political, moral, psychological and philosophical, and was variously lucid and opaque, incisive and ambiguous, its meanings and possibilities unfolded luxuriantly and extended tentacularly in time.

*

Given that some of the most clear, vivid and telling passages of the tale evoke sympathy for the Africans and scorn for the colonialists, and given that such satiric scorn was exceptional in 1899, how did it come about that eventually the tale could be accused, by postcolonial, Marxist and feminist writers, of racial prejudice, male chauvinism, and even pro-imperialism?

To Chinua Achebe, lecturing in 1975, 'Conrad was a bloody racist'. In 'Heart of Darkness', he claimed, the Africans are marginalised, dehumanised; Africa is reduced to 'the role of props for the breakup of one petty European mind'; and the result is 'an offensive and totally deplorable book'.[22] A year later, the Marxist critic, Terry Eagleton, declared:

> The 'message' of *Heart of Darkness* is that Western civilisation is at base as barbarous as African society – a viewpoint which disturbs imperialist assumptions to the precise degree that it reinforces them . . . . . Aesthetic form must vanquish the inchoate, as imperialism strives to subdue the 'disorganisation' of tribal

society to 'rational' structure; yet such ordering always contains its own negation.[23]

Soon, feminist critics assailed the work. Nina Pelikan Straus, Bette London, Johanna M. Smith and Elaine Showalter were among those who argued that 'Heart of Darkness' was both imperialist and sexist. Straus, for instance, declared:

> The woman reader . . . . . is in the position to insist that Marlow's cowardice consists of his inability to face the dangerous self that is the form of his own masculinist vulnerability: his own complicity in the racist, sexist, imperialistic, and finally libidinally satisfying world he has inhabited with Kurtz.[24]

Achebe's view was widely influential, though not all post-colonial critics of Conrad endorsed Achebe's sweeping condemnation of the tale. Lewis Nkosi, Mathew Buyu, Ngugi wa Thiong'o, Wilson Harris, C. P. Sarvan and Peter Nazareth inclined to the view that though Conrad was ambivalent in racial matters, 'Heart of Darkness' was progressive in its satiric account of the colonialists.[25] Sarvan concluded: 'Conrad . . . was not entirely immune to the infection of the beliefs and attitudes of his age, but he was ahead of most in trying to break free.' Frances B. Singh noted that though the tale was now vulnerable in several respects, including the association of Africans with supernatural evil, 'Heart of Darkness' should remain within 'the canon of works indicting colonialism'. Peter Nazareth, the Ugandan writer, said:

> Conrad was . . . . . a mental liberator: not only for those blinded at home but also for those who were to come later, the colonized elite wearing the eyes of Europe.

Such comments might also serve as a response to Eagleton.

The feminist critique is based largely on the fact that in the tale, a man (Marlow) tells a group of men a story about 'men's work' in Africa; women are implicitly and explicitly subordinated. Marlow says, for example:

> It's queer how out of touch with truth women are. They live in a world of their own . . . . . It is too beautiful altogether . . . . .[26]

Eventually, he lies to the Intended. It appears that men can and should have access to the truth, whereas women do not and should not. Marlow's aunt believes the imperialists' propaganda; the Intended remains trapped in her misguided faith in Kurtz. One of the tale's themes is Faustian: in contrast to the sceptical, relativistic features of the narrative are the hints of supernatural agency: Kurtz seems to have made a diabolical pact, exchanging his soul for power. Sometimes the jungle itself is virtually personified as the corrupting agency, and is feminised as a vampiric seductress:

> The wilderness .... had caressed him, and – lo! – he had withered; it had taken him, loved him, embraced him, got into his veins, consumed his flesh, and sealed his soul to its own by the inconceivable ceremonies of some devilish initiation.[27]

Kurtz's African consort is described in ways which intermittently suggest that she is an incarnation of the wilderness's power:

> [T]he colossal body of the fecund and mysterious life seemed to look at her as though it had been looking at the image of its own passionate and tenebrous soul ..... She stood looking at us without a stir, and like the wilderness itself with an air of brooding over an inscrutable purpose.[28]

Earlier, we had been told that the jungle's stillness 'was the stillness of an implacable force brooding over an inscrutable intention. It looked at you with a vengeful aspect.'[29] So, part of the time, the narrative suggests (with portentous rhetoric) that the jungle has a capacity to take vengeance on the European invaders, and that one agent of that retribution is the seductive woman.

'The Heart of Darkness' is such a complex tale that generalisations based on some parts of it can often be challenged by generalisations based on other parts. Marlow (whose words are reported by another character) is not fully reliable as narrator; his views are not necessarily Conrad's, nor are they consistent. In 1910 Conrad signed an open letter to the Prime Minister, Herbert Asquith, advocating votes for women.[30] Though the Marlow of 'The Heart of Darkness' says that women are out of touch with the trv h, the Marlow of *Chance* says that they know the whole truth but mercifully conceal it from men, who live in a 'fool's paradise'.[31] In 'The Heart of Darkness' females are depicted in diverse and contrasting ways: the African woman knows what the Intended does not; at the company's offices in the city, the two females who meet the applicants are mysterious and apparently knowing, even fateful. Marlow's aunt cannot be living entirely 'in a world of her own', for it is she whose influence with the company gains employment for her nephew. Almost all the white men described by Marlow seem to be involved in hypocrisy and corruption; they are participants in what appears to be the great lie of colonialism – exploitation claiming to be philanthropy.

*

The criticisms by Achebe, Eagleton and Straus raise a large question about the relationship between political evaluations and literary works. 'The Heart of Darkness' has many political aspects, but it is not a political manifesto. It is a fictional work designed to offer intelligent entertainment. It offers voluntary, hypothetical experiences: a magic of vicariousness in which the searching of reality depends on the reader's initial imaginative flight from reality. Literature is not a branch of politics: indeed, its rich, ambiguous, tentative features, combined with its linguistic resourcefulness, constantly challenge the relatively inflexible and dogmatic rhetoric of people for whom the political is a master-discourse. The tale may be scanned in a variety of ways, and each mode of scansion tends to give temporary prominence to some features of the tale while temporarily veiling others; few critics are able to maintain the multiple scansion which might do reasonable justice to the polyvalence of the text. Interpretative analysis may elucidate the meanings; but, inevitably (being functionally rationalistic in intent), it cannot provide an equivalent to the experience of the totality of the original work.

A standard political approach consists of summarising the work so as to elicit its apparent political message and of comparing that message with the political biases of the critic. To the extent that the work supports those biases, it is commended; to the extent that it opposes those biases, it is condemned. Such an approach may be very reductive, simplifying complexity and ambiguity; and it may be egoistic, since it implies the general validity of the critic's outlook, or upbraids the past for not endorsing the critical present.

'The Heart of Darkness' offers repeated warnings against such egoism. Marlow misinterprets signs and objects; his beliefs are shaken and changed by experience; and his narrative is challenged on at least two occasions by his hearers on the yawl. The suspense and vividness of the tale depend largely on the technique of delayed decoding, in which a marked delay occurs between an effect and the recognition of its cause, between an enigma and its explanation.[32] This is used on a small, medium and large scale. On a small scale, one example is the annotation in the manual of seamanship that Marlow finds. He infers that those marks are words in secret code, but he is wrong; eventually he learns that they are merely notes in Russian. On a medium scale, there is the matter of the wrecked steamboat. At first it seems to be a senseless accident, but gradually Marlow begins to perceive that the wrecking (like the shortage of rivets for the repair) has been contrived by the manager to delay Kurtz's relief. Here delayed decoding, sustained at length, becomes covert plotting: that is, when a plot-sequence is so elliptically presented that it may be perceived as a sequence only on a second or third reading of the text. On a large scale, Marlow's whole narrative is one large act of delayed decoding: for he, after an interval of years, is trying to comprehend the meanings of his journey into Africa; he is still casting around (by trial and error) to define them.

Typically, Marlow offers us a wide range of interpretations of Kurtz's words, 'The horror! The horror!'; a range so wide, indeed, that we may be left uncertain; the words retain a residue of the unknowable. Repeatedly on his journey, Marlow encounters events which are given the quality of vivid enigmas; some are resolved, others are not; and much of the fiercely satiric observation gives prominence to the fact that different individuals may see in radically different ways the same occurrences: Kurtz's 'methods', the fire at the central station, the quest for ivory, the conquest of Africa. Even one individual may veer in interpretation: Marlow presents his lie to the Intended as both 'a trifle' and symbolically immense. To a far greater extent than most previous tales, 'The Heart of Darkness' involves the reader in an adventure in interpretation which offers warnings of the pitfalls of interpretation. There is a lesson here for its critics.

In a great literary work, the readily paraphrasable is constantly challenged by the aesthetically entrancing, the linguistically sensuous, and the protean provisionality of the whole. Richly suggestive, densely compressed, astonishing in its concretely vivid combinations of the descriptive, the analytic and the symbolic, 'The Heart of Darkness' has resources of meaning and evocation that are unlikely to be exhausted by the interpretations of critics who necessarily are trapped in the limited discourse of non-fictional prose. To Marlow,

> the meaning of an episode was not inside like a kernel but outside, enveloping the tale which brought it out only as a glow brings out a haze . . .[33]

'The Heart of Darkness', we may conclude, will continue to project its intense glow through time and space.

CEDRIC WATTS

References

1. C. B. Cox: Introduction to Joseph Conrad, *Youth: A Narrative/Heart of Darkness/The End of the Tether* (London: Dent, 1974; repr. 1992), p. vii. Lionel Trilling, *Sincerity and Authenticity* (London: Oxford University Press, 1972), p. 106.

2. By 'Gothic' I refer to the tradition of Gothic fiction which includes Ann Radcliffe's *The Mysteries of Udolpho*, M. G. Lewis's *The Monk*, Emily Brontë's *Wuthering Heights* and Bram Stoker's *Dracula*. In these novels the supernatural and Satanic are either suggested but not endorsed (Radcliffe), presented ambiguously (Brontë), or fully endorsed (Lewis and Stoker). Some of the recurrent metaphors of 'The Heart of Darkness' intermittently recall this hinterland. Kurtz is termed a 'wraith' or 'phantom', says 'I have been dead – and damned', and craves 'more blood'. Marlow (p. 81) describes him as:

> that Shadow – this wandering and tormented thing, that seemed released from one grave only to sink for ever into another.

3. Henry Norman, 'The Globe and the Island', *Cosmopolis*, July 1897, p. 81.

4. *Joseph Conrad's Letters to R. B. Cunninghame Graham*, ed. C. T. Watts (London: Cambridge University Press, 1969), p. 126.

5. Thomas Carlyle, *Past and Present* [1843] (London: Chapman & Hall, 1858), p. 302. H. M. Stanley, quoting Carlyle, said that King Leopold was God's chosen instrument for redeeming the Congo.

6. *The Times*, 5 May 1898, p. 7. ('I should think Lord Salisbury's dying nation must be enjoying the fun', remarked Conrad.)

7. 'Geography and Some Explorers', *Last Essays* [1926] (London: Dent, 1955), p. 17.

8. In 'Autocracy and War' [1905], Conrad says, for example:

> The intellectual stage of mankind being as yet in its infancy, and States, like most individuals, having but a feeble and imperfect consciousness of the worth and force of the inner life, the need of making their existence manifest to themselves is determined in the direction of physical activity. The idea of ceasing to grow in territory, in strength, in wealth, in influence – in anything but wisdom and self-knowledge [–] is odious to them as the omen of the end.
>
> (*Notes on Life and Letters* [London: Dent, 1949], pp. 108–9.)

Conrad could also, however, write of that 'liberty, which can only be found under the English flag' (*The Collected Letters of Joseph Conrad*, ed. Frederick R. Karl and Laurence Davies, Vol. 2 [Cambridge: Cambridge University Press, 1986], p. 230). He veered between (a) regarding all imperialism as bad, (b) regarding British imperialism as the best of a bad lot, and (c) regarding British imperialism as the fine exception to the general rule.

9. Quoted in Maurice N. Hennessy, *Congo: A Brief History and Appraisal* (London and Dunmow: Pall Mall Press, 1961), p. 13. Guy Burrows, *The Land of the Pigmies*, (London: Pearson, 1898), p. 286.

10. Conrad's letters to Casement are published in *The Collected Letters of Joseph Conrad*, Vol. 3 (1988), pp. 87, 95–7, 103, 161–2.

11. *The Collected Letters of Joseph Conrad*, Vol. 3, pp. 96–7. When supplying the statement, Conrad told Casement: 'Once more my best wishes go with you on your crusade. Of course You may make any use you like of what I write to you.' Conrad assailed Leopold in *The Inheritors* (1901), written jointly with F. M. Hueffer.

12. *King Leopold's Rule in Africa* (London: Heinemann, 1904), p. 351–2, *Morning Post*, 12 October 1904, p. 8.

13. Letter of 7 October 1909, quoted in W. R. Louis and Jean Stengers, *E. D. Morel's History of the Congo Reform Movement* (London: Oxford University Press, 1968), p. 205.

14. In 1908 Leopold acquiesced in the transference of control of the Congo to the Belgian government by an act of annexation. Gradually, conditions in the region improved (see Neil Ascherson, *The King Incorporated* [London: Allen & Unwin, 1963], p. 281). When the Congo Reform Association, in 1913, formally ended its campaign, Morel declared that most of its aims had been achieved: 'The native of the Congo is once more a free man ... The rubber-tax – "the blood tax" – has been abolished.' (*E. D. Morel's History of the Congo Reform Movement*, p. 206.)
  The Congo gained independence in 1960, and in 1971 its name became Zaïre. A century after Conrad's journey there, corruption, disorder and poverty were widespread.

15. Hunt Hawkins, 'Joseph Conrad, Roger Casement, and the Congo Reform Movement', *Journal of Modern Literature*, 9 (1981), p. 80.

16. Cunninghame Graham had sent Conrad his satiric essay, 'Bloody Niggers' (*The Social-Democrat*, 1, April 1897, pp. 104–9), which denounced racial prejudice in general and the pejorative term 'niggers' in particular. Conrad commented: 'Very good, very telling ...' (*Joseph Conrad's Letters to R. B. Cunninghame Graham*, p. 89).

17. See 'The Heart of Darkness', pp. 15–16.

18. *Ibid.*, pp. 16.

19. *Ibid.*, p. 18.

20. *Ibid.*, p. 7.

21. 'Heart of Darkness' provides the epigraph of Eliot's 'The Hollow Men': 'Mistah Kurtz – he dead'. For *The Waste Land*, Eliot's original choice of epigraph (which he deemed 'much the most appropriate ... and somewhat elucidative') was a passage from the tale culminating in Kurtz's words, 'The horror! The horror!' (See *The Waste Land*, ed. Valerie Eliot [London: Faber & Faber, 1971], p. 2.) Greene admired Conrad's work generally, and a 'Mr Kurtz' appears in his tale 'The Third Man'. On his own journey into the Congo he took 'Heart of Darkness' with him as a reference-point ('still a fine story' even if 'its faults show now'), and, reflecting on Conrad's device of comparing the concrete to the abstract, remarked: 'Is this a trick that I have caught?' (*In Search of a Character* [London: Bodley Head, 1961], p. 51).

22. 'An Image of Africa' [lecture given in 1975]: *Massachusetts Review*, 18 (1977), pp. 788, 790.

23. *Criticism and Ideology: A Study in Marxist Literary Theory* (London: New Left Books, 1976; repr. London: Verso, 1978), pp. 135, 137. See also: Steve Smith: 'Marxism and Ideology: Joseph Conrad's *Heart of Darkness*' in *Literary Theory at Work: Three Texts*, ed. Douglas Tallack (London: Batsford; Totowa, N. J.: Barnes & Noble; 1987); and Brook Thomas: 'Preserving and Keeping Order by Killing Time in *Heart of Darkness*' in *Joseph Conrad: 'Heart of Darkness': A Case Study in Contemporary Criticism*, ed. Ross C. Murfin (New York: St Martin's Press, 1989).

24. 'The Exclusion of the Intended from Secret Sharing in Conrad's *Heart of Darkness*': *Novel*, 20 (1987), p. 135.

25. Lewis Nkosi, conversation with me, and brief comment in his *Tasks and Masks* (Harlow: Longman, 1981), p. 80. Mathew Buyu, 'Racial Intercourse in Conrad's Malaysian and African Fiction' (unpublished D.Phil. thesis, 1987, Sussex University Library). *Heart of Darkness*, ed. Robert Kimbrough (3rd edn: New York and London: Norton, 1988), p. 285 (Ngugi), pp. 262–8 (Harris), pp. 280–5 (Sarvan), pp. 268–80 (Singh; quotation, p. 280). Nazareth, 'Out of Darkness: Conrad and Other Third World Writers': *Conradiana*, 14 (1982), pp. 173–87; quotation, p. 178.

26. 'The Heart of Darkness', p. 14.

27. *Ibid.*, p. 58.

28. *Ibid.*, p. 75.

29. *Ibid.*, p. 4.

30. Reported in *The Times*, 15 June 1910, p. 7. The list of signatories included Cunninghame Graham, Sarah Grand, Bernard Shaw and May Sinclair. See also: *The Collected Letters of Joseph Conrad*, Vol. 4 (1990), p. 327.

31. *Chance* (London: Methuen, 1914), p. 131.

32. See Ian Watt, *Conrad in the Nineteenth Century* (London: Chatto & Windus, 1980), pp. 175–9; Cedric Watts, *The Deceptive Text* (Brighton: Harvester, 1984), pp. 43–6, 119–20.

33. 'The Heart of Darkness', p. 6.

NOTE ON THE TEXT

This tale by Conrad was first published as a serial: in *Blackwood's Edinburgh Magazine*, Vol. 165, pp. 193–220, 479–502, 634–57: February, March and April, 1899. There, the title was 'The Heart of Darkness'.

More than three years later, the tale was first incorporated in a book, as part of *Youth: A Narrative / and / Two Other Stories* (Edinburgh and London: Blackwood, November 1902). Its title there, and thereafter, was simply 'Heart of Darkness'. Of the numerous other differences between the serial text and the book text, some are relatively important (see below), others relatively trivial.

The copy-text used for this 1995 Everyman edition is the original, published in *Blackwood's Magazine*. Readers thus see the version which appeared in the reign of Victoria and before the Boer War had begun; a version more radical (because of its Victorian context) than the later editions. This, therefore, is a text with specific historic credentials, and not a combination of material from a variety of dates and editions.

My emendations to the original text are few. They are listed here, so that readers may, if they wish, reconstitute the original 'warts and all'. Page numbers refer to this 1995 Everyman edition; the 1899 reading is enclosed in square brackets. I have added the heading 'PART I' at the tale's opening, since *Blackwood's Magazine* numbered the subsequent part (now headed 'PART II') as 'II.'; and I have put 'PART III' where *Blackwood's* has 'CONCLUSION.'

    16   drooped [dropped]
    19   moved, [moved]
    31   mâché [maché]
    37   PART II [II.]
    55   lunged [lounged]
    67   PART III [CONCLUSION.]
    85   ratchets [rachets]

A selection of the main differences between the *Blackwood's Magazine* text and the 1902 text is given below. (Again, page numbers refer to this Everyman edition.) The original version offers a fuller response to Kurtz's African consort, makes Kurtz's depravity more explicit, and gives stronger emphasis to the Intended's truthful appearance.

p. 38: ill – had recovered . . .
1902: ill – had recovered imperfectly . . .

p. 69: There was no sign on the face of nature of this amazing tale of cruelty and greed that . . . . .
1902: There was no sign on the face of nature of this amazing tale that . . .

p. 70: These round knobs were not ornamental but symbolic; they were symbolic of some cruel and forbidden knowledge. They were expressive . . . .
1902: These round knobs were not ornamental but symbolic; they were expressive . . . .

p. 71: invasion. It had tempted him with all the sinister suggestions of its loneliness. I think . . . . .
1902: invasion. I think . . .

p. 75: And we men also looked at her – at any rate I looked at her. She came abreast . . . . .
1902: She came abreast . . . . .

p. 75: she stopped. Had her heart failed her, or had her eyes, veiled with that mournfulness that lies over all the wild things of the earth, seen the hopelessness of longing that will find out sometimes even a savage soul in the lonely darkness of its being? Who can tell. Perhaps she did not know herself. The young fellow . . . . .

1902: she stopped as if her heart had failed her. The young fellow . . . . .

p. 75: embrace. Her sudden gesture seemed to demand a cry, but the unbroken silence that hung over the scene was more formidable than any sound could be.

1902: embrace. A formidable silence hung over the scene.

p. 81: this wandering and tormented thing, that seemed released from one grave only to sink for ever into another.

1902: this wandering and tormented thing.

p. 82: No eloquence could have been so withering as his final burst of sincerity.

1902: No eloquence could have been so withering to one's belief in mankind as his final burst of sincerity.

p. 83: "I will return," he said, slowly, . . .

1902: 'Do I not?' he said slowly, ...

p. 85: a veil had been rent. I saw on that ivory face the expression of strange pride, of mental power, of avarice, of blood-thirstiness, of cunning, of excessive terror, of an intense and hopeless despair. Did he live his life through in every detail . . . . .

1902: a veil had been rent. I saw on that ivory face the expression of sombre pride, of ruthless power, of craven terror, of an intense and hopeless despair. Did he live his life again in every detail . . . . .

p. 86: man who had so unhesitatingly pronounced a judgment . . . . .

1902: man who had pronounced a judgment . . . . .

pp. 89–90: yet that face on paper seemed to be a reflection of truth itself. One felt that no manipulation of light and pose could have conveyed the delicate shade of truthfulness upon those features. She looked out truthfully. She seemed ready . . . . .

1902: yet one felt that no manipulation of light and pose could have conveyed the delicate shade of truthfulness upon those features. She seemed ready . . . . .

pp. 90–91: simplicity: "I have lived – supremely!" "What do you want here? I have been dead – and damned." "Let me go – I want more of it."

More of what? More blood, more heads on stakes, more adoration, rapine, and murder. I remembered . . . . .
1902: simplicity. I remembered . . . . .

p. 92: behold. I wanted to get out. She . . . . .
1902: behold. She . . .

p. 93: lamp. But in the box I had brought to his bedside there were several packages pretty well alike, all tied with shoe-strings, and probably he had made a mistake. And the girl . . . . .
1902: lamp. And the girl . . . . .

For this 1995 edition, Everyman has made the following conventional changes to the original Blackwood 'house style'. A punctuation mark which follows an italicised word is not italicised, and some punctuation marks which were originally placed within quotations are now placed after them. Where the original text used double quotation marks, this text uses single ones, and *vice versa*. An asterisk in the text indicates a note at the end.

In quotations which appear in the editorial matter of this volume, a row of five points (. . . . .) represents an omission that *I* have made, whereas a row of three points represents an ellipsis already present in the material being quoted. Any other changes to quoted material are enclosed within square brackets.

THE HEART OF DARKNESS*

PART I

The *Nellie*, a cruising yawl, swung to her anchor without a flutter of the sails, and was at rest.* The flood had made, the wind was nearly calm, and being bound down the river, the only thing for us was to come to and wait for the turn of the tide.

The sea-reach of the Thames stretched before us like the beginning of an interminable waterway. In the offing the sea and the sky were welded together without a joint, and in the luminous space the tanned sails of the barges drifting up with the tide seemed to stand still in red clusters of canvas sharply peaked, with gleams of varnished sprits. A haze rested on the low shores that ran out to sea in vanishing flatness. The air was dark above Gravesend, and farther back still seemed condensed into a mournful gloom, brooding motionless over the biggest, and the greatest, town on earth.

The Director of Companies was our captain and our host. We four affectionately watched his back as he stood in the bows looking to seaward. On the whole river there was nothing that looked half so nautical. He resembled a pilot, which to a seaman is trustworthiness personified. It was difficult to realise his work was not out there in the luminous estuary, but behind him, within the brooding gloom.

Between us there was, as I have already said somewhere,* the bond of the sea. Besides holding our hearts together through long periods of separation it had the effect of making us tolerant of each other's yarns – and even convictions. The Lawyer – the best of old fellows – had, because of his many years and many virtues, the only cushion on deck, and was lying on the only rug. The Accountant had brought out already a box of dominoes, and was toying architecturally with the bones.* Marlow sat cross-legged right aft, leaning against the mizzen-mast. He had sunken cheeks, a yellow complexion, a straight back, an ascetic aspect, and, with his arms dropped, the palms of hands outwards, resembled an idol. The Director, satisfied the anchor had good hold, made his way aft and sat down amongst us. We exchanged a few words lazily. Afterwards there was silence on board the yacht. For some reason or other we did not begin that game of dominoes. We felt meditative, and fit for nothing but placid staring. The day was ending in a serenity that had a still and exquisite brilliance. The water shone pacifically; the sky, without a speck, was a benign immensity of unstained light; the very mist on the Essex marshes was like a gauzy and radiant fabric, hung from the wooded rises inland, and draping the low shores in diaphanous folds. Only the gloom to the west, brooding over the upper reaches, became more sombre every minute, as if angered by the approach of the sun.

And at last, in its curved and imperceptible fall, the sun sank low, and from glowing white changed to a dull red without rays and without heat, as if about to go out suddenly, stricken to death by the touch of that gloom brooding over a crowd of men.

Forthwith a change came over the waters, and the serenity became less brilliant but more profound. The old river in its broad reach rested unruffled at the decline of day, after ages of good service done to the race that peopled its banks, spread out in the tranquil dignity of a waterway leading to the uttermost ends of the earth. We looked at the venerable stream not in the vivid flush of a short day that comes and departs for ever, but in the pacific yet august light of abiding memories. And indeed nothing is easier for a man who has, as the phrase goes, 'followed the sea' with reverence and affection, than to evoke the great spirit of the past upon the lower reaches of the Thames. The tidal current runs to and fro in its unceasing service, crowded with memories of men and ships it had borne to the rest of home or to the battles of the sea. It had known and served all the men of whom the nation is proud, from Sir Francis Drake to Sir John Franklin, knights all, titled and untitled – the great knights-errant of the sea. It had borne all the ships whose names are like jewels flashing in the night of time, from the *Golden Hind* returning with her round flanks full of treasure, to be visited by the Queen's Highness and thus pass out of the gigantic tale, to the *Erebus* and *Terror*, bound on other conquests – and that never returned.* It had known the ships and the men. They sailed from Deptford, from Greenwich, from Erith, the adventurers and the settlers; kings' ships and the ships of men on 'Change; captains, admirals, the dark 'interlopers' of the Eastern trade, and the commissioned 'generals' of East India fleets.* Hunters for gold or pursuers of fame, they all had gone out on that stream, bearing the sword, and often the torch, messengers of the might within the land, bearers of a spark from the sacred fire. What greatness had not floated on the ebb of that river into the mystery of an unknown earth? – the dreams of men, the seed of commonwealths, the germs of empires.

The sun set; the dusk fell on the stream, and lights began to appear along the shore. The Chapman lighthouse, a three-legged thing erect on a mudflat, shone strongly. Lights of ships moved in the fairway – a great stir of lights going up and going down. And farther west on the upper reaches the place of the monstrous town was still marked ominously on the sky, a brooding gloom in sunshine, a lurid glare under the stars.

'And this also,' said Marlow suddenly, 'has been one of the dark places of the earth.'*

He was the only man of us who still 'followed the sea'. The worst that could be said of him was that he did not represent his class. He was a seaman, but he was a wanderer too, while most seamen lead, if one may so express it, a sedentary life. Their minds are of the stay-at-home order, and their home is always with them – the ship; and so is their country – the sea. One ship is very much like another, and the sea is always the same. In the immutability of their surroundings the foreign shores, the foreign faces, the changing immensity of life, glide past, veiled not by a sense of mystery but by a slightly disdainful ignorance; for there is nothing mysterious to a seaman unless it be the sea itself, which is the mistress of his existence and as inscrutable as Destiny. For the rest, after his hours of work a casual stroll or a casual spree on shore suffices to unfold for him the secret of a whole continent, and generally he finds the secret not worth knowing. The yarns of seamen have a direct simplicity, the whole meaning of which lies within the shell of a cracked nut. But Marlow was not typical (if his propensity to spin yarns be excepted), and to him the meaning of an episode was not inside like a kernel but outside, enveloping the tale which brought it out only as a glow brings out a haze, in the likeness of one of these misty halos that sometimes are made visible by the spectral illumination of moonshine.

His uncalled-for remark did not seem at all surprising. It was just like Marlow. It was accepted in silence. No one took the trouble to grunt even; and presently he said, very slow,—

'I was thinking of very old times, when the Romans first came here,* nineteen hundred years ago – the other day . . . Light came out of this river since – you say Knights?* Yes; but it is like a running blaze on a plain, like a flash of lighting in the clouds. We live in the flicker – may it last as long as the old earth keeps rolling! But darkness was here yesterday. Imagine the feelings of a commander of a fine – what d'ye call 'em? – trireme in the Mediterranean, ordered suddenly to the north; run overland across the Gauls in a hurry; put in charge of one of these craft the legionaries, – a wonderful lot of handy men they must have been too – used to build, apparently by the hundred, in a month or two, if we may believe what we read.* Imagine him here – the very end of the world, a sea the colour of lead, a sky the colour of smoke, a kind of ship about as rigid as a concertina – and going up this river with stores, or orders, or what you like. Sandbanks, marshes, forests, savages, – precious little to eat fit for a civilised man, nothing but Thames water to drink. No Falernian wine here, no going ashore. Here and there a military camp lost in a wilderness, like a needle in a bundle of hay – cold, fog, tempests, disease, exile, and death, – death skulking in the air, in the water, in the bush. They must have been dying like flies here. Oh yes – he did it. Did it very well, too, no doubt, and without thinking much about it either, except afterwards to brag of what he had gone through in his time, perhaps. They were men enough to face the darkness. And perhaps he was cheered by keeping his eye on a chance of promotion to the fleet at Ravenna by-and-by, if he had good friends in Rome and survived the awful climate. Or think of a

decent young citizen in a toga – perhaps too much dice, you know
– coming out here in the train of some prefect, or tax-gatherer, or
trader even, to mend his fortunes.* Land in a swamp, march
through the woods, and in some inland post feel the savagery, the
utter savagery, had closed round him, – all that mysterious life of
the wilderness that stirs in the forest, in the jungles, in the hearts of
wild men. There's no initiation either into such mysteries. He has
to live in the midst of the incomprehensible, which is also
detestable. And it has a fascination, too, that goes to work upon
him. The fascination of the abomination – you know. Imagine the
growing regrets, the longing to escape, the powerless disgust, the
surrender, the hate.'

He paused.

'Mind,' he began again, lifting one arm from the elbow, the
palm of the hand outwards, so that, with his legs folded before
him, he had the pose of a Buddha preaching in European clothes
and without a lotus-flower* – 'Mind, none of us would feel
exactly like this. What saves us is efficiency – the devotion to
efficiency.* But these chaps were not much account, really. They
were no colonists; their administration was merely a squeeze, and
nothing more, I suspect. They were conquerors, and for that you
want only brute force – nothing to boast of, when you have it,
since your strength is just an accident arising from the weakness of
others. They grabbed what they could get for the sake of what was
to be got.* It was just robbery with violence, aggravated murder
on a great scale, and men going at it blind – as is very proper for
those who tackle a darkness. The conquest of the earth, which
mostly means the taking it away from those who have a different
complexion or slightly flatter noses than ourselves, is not a pretty
thing when you look into it too much. What redeems it is the idea
only. An idea at the back of it; not a sentimental pretence but an
idea; and an unselfish belief in the idea – something you can set
up, and bow down before, and offer a sacrifice to . . .'

He broke off. Flames glided in the river, small green flames, red
flames, white flames, pursuing, overtaking, joining, crossing each
other – then separating slowly or hastily.* The traffic of the great
city went on in the deepening night upon the sleepless river.* We

looked on, waiting patiently – there was nothing else to do till the end of the flood; but it was only after a long silence, when he said, in a hesitating voice, 'I suppose you fellows remember I did once turn fresh-water sailor for a bit,' that we knew we were fated, before the ebb began to run, to hear about one of Marlow's inconclusive experiences.

'I don't want to bother you much with what happened to me personally,' he began, showing in this remark the weakness of many tellers of tales who seem so often unaware of what their audience would best like to hear; 'yet to understand the effect of it on me you ought to know how I got out there, what I saw, how I went up that river to the place where I first met the poor chap. It was the farthest point of navigation and the culminating point of my experience. It seemed somehow to throw a kind of light on everything about me – and into my thoughts. It was sombre enough too – and pitiful – not extraordinary in any way – not very clear either. No, not very clear. And yet it seemed to throw a kind of light.

'I had then, as you remember, just returned to London after a lot of Indian Ocean, Pacific, China Seas – a regular dose of the East – six years or so, and I was loafing about, hindering you fellows in your work and invading your homes, just as though I had got a heavenly mission to civilise you. It was very fine for a time, but after a bit I did get tired of resting. Then I began to look for a ship – I should think the hardest work on earth. But the ships wouldn't even look at me. And I got tired of that game too.

'Now when I was a little chap I had a passion for maps. I would look for hours at South America, or Africa, or Australia, and lose myself in all the glories of exploration. At that time there were many blank spaces on the earth, and when I saw one that looked particularly inviting on a map (but they all look that) I would put my finger on it and say, When I grow up I will go there.* The North Pole was one of these places, I remember. Well, I haven't been there yet, and shall not try now. The glamour's off. Other places were scattered about the Equator, and in every sort of latitude all over the two hemispheres. I have been in some of them, and . . . well, we won't talk about that. But there was one yet – the biggest, the most blank, so to speak – that I had a hankering after.

'True, by this time it was not a blank space any more. It had got filled since my boyhood with rivers and lakes and names. It had ceased to be a blank space of delightful mystery – a white patch for a boy to dream gloriously over.* It had become a place of darkness. But there was in it one river especially, a mighty big river, that you could see on the map, resembling an immense snake uncoiled, with its head in the sea, its body at rest curving afar over a vast country, and its tail lost in the depths of the land. And as I looked at the map of it in a shop-window, it fascinated me as a snake would a bird – a silly little bird. Then I remembered there was a big concern, a Company for trade on that river.* Dash it all! I thought to myself, they can't trade without using some kind of craft on that lot of fresh water – steam-boats! Why shouldn't I try to get charge of one. I went on along Fleet Street, but could not shake off the idea. The snake had charmed me.

'You understand it was a Continental concern, that Trading society; but I have a lot of relations living on the Continent, because it's cheap and not so nasty as it looks, they say.

'I am sorry to own I began to worry them. This was already a fresh departure for me. I was not used to get things that way, you know. I always went my own road and on my own legs where I had a mind to go. I wouldn't have believed it of myself; but, then – you see – I felt somehow I must get there by hook or by crook. So I worried them. The men said "My dear fellow," and did nothing. Then – would you believe it? – I tried the women. I, Charlie Marlow, set the women to work – to get a job. Heavens! Well, you see, the notion drove me. I had an aunt, a dear enthusiastic soul.* She wrote: "It will be delightful. I am ready to do anything, anything for you. It is a glorious idea. I know the wife of a very high personage in the Administration, and also a man who has lots of influence with," etc., etc. She was determined to make no end of fuss to get me appointed skipper of a river steam-boat, if such was my fancy.

'I got my appointment – of course; and I got it very quick. It appears the Company had received news that one of their captains had been killed in a scuffle with the natives. This was my chance, and it made me the more anxious to go. It was only months and months afterwards, when I made the attempt to recover what was left of the body, that I heard the original quarrel arose from a misunderstanding about some hens. Yes, two black hens. Fresleven* – that was the fellow's name, a Dane – thought himself wronged somehow in the bargain, so he went ashore and started to hammer the chief of the village with a stick. Oh, it didn't surprise me in the least to hear this, and at the same time to be told that Fresleven was the gentlest, quietest creature that ever walked on two legs. No doubt he was; but he had been a couple of years already out there engaged in the noble cause, you know, and he probably felt the need at last of asserting his self-respect in some way. Therefore he whacked the old nigger mercilessly, while a big crowd of his people watched him, thunderstruck, till some man, – I was told the chief's son, – in desperation at hearing the old chap yell, made a tentative jab with a spear at the white man – and of course it went quite easy between the shoulder-blades. Then the whole population cleared into the forest, expecting all kinds of calamities to happen, while, on the other hand, the steamer Fresleven commanded left also in a bad panic, in charge of the engineer, I believe. Afterwards nobody seemed to trouble much about Fresleven's remains, till I got out and stepped into his shoes. I couldn't let it rest, though; but when an opportunity offered at last to meet my predecessor, the grass growing through his ribs was tall enough to hide his bones. They were all there. The supernatural being had not been touched after he fell. And the village was deserted, the huts gaped black, rotting, all askew within the fallen enclosures. A calamity had come to it, sure enough. The people had vanished. Mad terror had scattered them, men, women, and children, through the bush, and they had never returned. What became of the hens I don't know either. I should think the cause of progress got them, anyhow. However, through this glorious affair I got my appointment, before I had fairly begun to hope for it.

'I flew around like mad to get ready, and before forty-eight hours I was crossing the Channel to show myself to my employers, and sign the contract. In a very few hours I arrived in a city that always makes me think of a whited sepulchre.* Prejudice no doubt. I had no difficulty in finding the Company's offices. It was the biggest thing in the town, and everybody I met was full of it. They were going to run an over-sea empire, and make no end of coin by trade.

'A narrow and deserted street in deep shadow, high houses, innumerable windows with venetian blinds, a dead silence, grass sprouting between the stones, imposing carriage archways right and left, immense double doors standing ponderously ajar. I slipped through one of these cracks, went up a swept and ungarnished staircase, as arid as a desert, and opened the first door I came to. Two women, one fat and the other slim, sat on straw-bottomed chairs, knitting black wool.* The slim one got up and walked straight at me – still knitting with downcast eyes – and only just as I began to think of getting out of her way, as you would for a somnambulist, stood still, and looked up. Her dress was as plain as an umbrella-cover, and she turned round without a word and preceded me into a waiting-room. I gave my name, and looked about. Deal table in the middle, plain chairs all round the walls, on one end a large shining map, marked with all the colours of a rainbow. There was a vast amount of red – good to see at any time, because one knows that some real work is done in there,* a deuce of a lot of blue, a little green, smears of orange, and, on the East Coast, a purple patch, to show where the jolly pioneers of progress drink the jolly lager-beer. However, I wasn't going into any of these. I was going into the yellow.* Dead in the centre. And the river was there – fascinating – deadly – like a snake. Ough! A door opened, a white-haired secretarial head, but wearing a compassionate expression, appeared, and a skinny forefinger beckoned me into the sanctuary. Its light was dim, and a heavy writing desk squatted in the middle. From behind that structure came out an impression of pale plumpness in a frock-coat.* The great man himself. He was five feet six, I should judge, and had his grip on the handle-end of ever so many millions. He shook hands, I fancy, murmured vaguely, was satisfied with my French. *Bon voyage.*

'In about forty-five seconds I found myself again in the waiting-room with the compassionate secretary, who, full of desolation and sympathy, made me sign some document. I believe I undertook amongst other things not to disclose any trade secrets.* Well, I am not going to.

'I began to feel slightly uneasy. You know I am not used to such ceremonies, and there was something ominous in the atmosphere. It was just as though I had been let into some conspiracy — I don't know — something not quite right; and I was glad to get out. In the outer room the two women knitted black wool feverishly. People were arriving, and the younger one was walking back and forth introducing them. The old one sat on her chair. Her flat cloth slippers were propped up on a foot-warmer, and a cat reposed on her lap. She wore a starched white affair on her head, had a wart on one cheek, and silver-rimmed spectacles hung on the tip of her nose. She glanced at me above the glasses. The swift and indifferent placidity of that look troubled me. Two youths with foolish and cheery countenances were being piloted over, and she threw at them the same quick glance of unconcerned wisdom. She seemed to know all about them and about me too. An eerie feeling came over me. She seemed uncanny and fateful. Often far away there I thought of these two, guarding the door of Darkness, knitting black wool as for a warm pall, one introducing, introducing, continuously to the unknown, the other scrutinising the cheery and foolish faces with unconcerned old eyes. *Ave!* Old knitter of black wool. *Morituri te salutant.** Not many of these she looked at ever saw her again — not half, by a long way.

'There was yet a visit to the doctor. "A simple formality," assured me the secretary,* with an air of taking an immense part in all my sorrows. Accordingly a young chap wearing his hat over the left eyebrow, some clerk I suppose, — there must have been clerks in the business, though the house was as still as a house in a city of the dead, — came from somewhere up-stairs, and led me forth. He was shabby and careless, with ink-stains on the sleeves of his jacket, and his cravat was large and billowy, under a chin shaped like the toe of an old boot. It was a little too early for the doctor, so I proposed a drink, and thereupon he developed a vein of joviality. As we sat over our vermuths he glorified the Company's business, and by-and-by I expressed casually my surprise at him not going out there. He became very cool and collected all at once. "I am not such a fool as I look, quoth Plato to his disciples," he said sententiously, emptied his glass with great resolution, and we rose.

'The old doctor felt my pulse, evidently thinking of something else the while. "Good, good for there," he mumbled, and then with a certain eagerness asked me whether I would let him measure my head.* Rather surprised, I said Yes, when he produced a thing like calipers and got the dimensions back and front and every way, taking notes carefully. He was an unshaven little man in a threadbare coat like a gaberdine, with his feet in slippers, and I thought him a harmless fool. "I always ask leave, in the interests of science, to measure the crania of those going out there," he said. "And when they come back too?" I asked. "Oh, I never see them," he remarked; "and, moreover, the changes take place inside, you know." He smiled, as if at some quiet joke. "So you are going out there. Famous. Interesting too." He gave me a searching glance, and made another note. "Ever any madness in your family?" he asked, in a matter-of-fact tone. I felt very annoyed. "Is that question in the interests of science too?" "It would be," he said, without taking notice of my irritation, "interesting for science to watch the mental changes of individuals, on the spot, but . . ." "Are you an alienist?" I interrupted. "Every doctor should be − a little," answered that original, imperturbably. "I have a little theory which you Messieurs who go out there must help me to prove. This is my share in the advantages my country shall reap from the possession of such a magnificent dependency. The mere wealth I leave to others. Pardon my questions, but you are the first Englishman coming under my observation . . ." I hastened to assure him I was not in the least typical. "If I were," said I, "I wouldn't be talking like this with you." "What you say is rather profound, and probably erroneous," he said, with a laugh. "Avoid irritation more than exposure to the sun. Adieu. How do you English say, eh? Good-bye. Ah! Good-bye. Adieu. In the tropics one must before everything keep calm.". . . He lifted a warning forefinger . . . "*Du calme, du calme. Adieu.*"

One thing more remained to do – say good-bye to my excellent aunt. I found her triumphant. I had a cup of tea – the last decent cup of tea for many days; and in a room that most soothingly looked just as you would expect a lady's drawing-room to look, we had a long quiet chat by the fireside. In the course of these confidences it became quite plain to me I had been represented to the wife of the high dignitary, and goodness knows to how many more people besides, as an exceptional and gifted creature – a piece of good fortune for the Company – a man you don't get hold of every day. Good heavens! and I was going to take charge of a two-penny-halfpenny river-steamboat with a penny whistle attached! It appeared, however, I was also one of the Workers, with a capital – you know.* Something like an emissary of light, something like a lower sort of apostle. There had been a lot of such rot let loose in print and talk just about that time,* and the excellent woman, living right in the rush of all that humbug, got carried off her feet. She talked about "weaning those ignorant millions from their horrid ways," till, upon my word, she made me quite uncomfortable. I ventured to hint that the Company was run for profit.

' "You forget, dear Charlie, that the labourer is worthy of his hire," she said, brightly.* It's queer how out of touch with truth women are. They live in a world of their own, and there had never been anything like it, and never can be. It is too beautiful altogether, and if they were to set it up it would go to pieces before the first sunset. Some confounded fact we men have been living contentedly with ever since the day of creation would start up and knock the whole thing over.*

'After this I got embraced, told to wear flannel, be sure to write often, and so on – and I left. In the street – I don't know why – a queer feeling came to me that I was an impostor. Odd thing that I, who used to clear out for any part of the world at twenty-four hours' notice, with less thought than most men give to the crossing of a street, had a moment – I won't say of hesitation, but of startled pause, before this commonplace affair. The best way I can explain it to you is by saying that, for a second or two, I felt as though, instead of going to the centre of a continent, I were about to set off for the centre of the earth.

'I left in a French steamer, and she called in every blamed port they have out there, for, as far as I could see, the sole purpose of landing soldiers and custom-house officers. I watched the coast. Watching a coast as it slips by the ship is like thinking about an enigma. There it is before you – smiling, frowning, inviting, grand, mean, insipid, or savage, and always mute with an air of whispering, Come and find out. This one was almost featureless, as if still in the making, with an aspect of monotonous grimness. The edge of a colossal jungle, so dark-green as to be almost black, fringed with white surf, ran straight, like a ruled line, far, far away along a blue sea whose glitter was blurred by a creeping mist. The sun was fierce, the land seemed to glisten and drip with steam. Here and there greyish-whitish specks showed up, clustered inside the white surf, with a flag flying above them perhaps. Settlements some centuries old, and still no bigger than pinheads on the untouched expanse of their background. We pounded along, stopped, landed soldiers; went on, landed custom-house clerks to levy toll in what looked like a God-forsaken wilderness, with a tin shed and a flag-pole lost in it; landed more soldiers – to take care of the custom-house clerks, presumably. Some, I heard, got drowned in the surf; but whether they did or not, nobody seemed particularly to care. They were just flung out there, and on we went. Every day the coast looked the same, as though we had not moved; but we passed various places – trading places – with names like Gran' Bassam, Little Popo, names that seemed to belong to some sordid farce acted in front of a sinister backcloth.* The idleness of a passenger, my isolation amongst all these men with whom I had no point of contact, the oily and languid sea, the uniform sombreness of the coast, seemed to keep me away from the truth of things within the toil of a mournful and senseless delusion. The voice of the surf heard now and then was a positive pleasure, like the speech of a brother. It was something natural, that had its reason, that had a meaning. Now and then a boat from the shore gave one a momentary contact with reality. It was paddled by black fellows. You could see from afar the white of their eye-balls glistening. They shouted, sang; their bodies streamed with perspiration; they had faces like grotesque masks

– these chaps; but they had bone, muscle, a wild vitality, an intense energy of movement, that was as natural and true as the surf along their coast. They wanted no excuse for being there. They were a great comfort to look at. For a time I would feel I belonged still to a world of straightforward facts; but the feeling would not last long. Something would turn up to scare it away. Once, I remember, we came upon a man-of-war anchored off the coast. There wasn't even a shed there, and she was shelling the bush. It appears the French had one of their wars going on thereabouts.* Her ensign drooped limp like a rag; the muzzles of the long eight- inch guns stuck out all over the low hull; the greasy, slimy swell swung her up lazily and let her down, swaying her thin masts. In the empty immensity of earth, sky, and water, there she was, incomprehensible, firing into a continent. Pop, would go one of the eight-inch guns; a small flame would dart and vanish, a little white smoke would disappear, a tiny projectile would give a feeble screech – and nothing happened. Nothing could happen. There was a touch of insanity in the proceeding, a sense of lugubrious drollery in the sight; and it was not dissipated by somebody on board assuring me earnestly there was a camp of natives – he called them enemies! – hidden out of sight somewhere.

'We gave her her letters (I heard the men in that lonely ship were dying of fever at the rate of three a-day) and went on. We called at some more places with farcical names, where the merry dance of death and trade goes on in a still and earthy atmosphere as of an overheated catacomb; all along the formless coast bordered by dangerous surf, as if Nature herself had tried to ward off intruders; in and out of rivers, streams of death in life, whose banks were rotting into mud, whose waters, thickened into slime, invaded the contorted mangroves, that seemed to writhe at us in the extremity of an impotent despair. Nowhere did we stop long enough to get a particularised impression, but the general sense of vague and oppressive wonder grew upon me. It was like a weary pilgrimage amongst hints for nightmares.

'It was upward of thirty days before I saw the mouth of the big river. We anchored off the seat of the government.* But my work would not begin till some two hundred miles farther on. So as soon as I could I made a start for a place thirty miles higher up.

'I had my passage on a little sea-going steamer. Her captain was a Swede, and knowing me for a seaman, invited me on the bridge. He was a young man, lean, fair, and morose, with lanky hair and a shuffling gait. As we left the miserable little wharf, he tossed his head contemptuously at the shore. "Been living there?" he asked. I said, "Yes." "Fine lot these government chaps — are they not?" he went on, speaking English with great precision and considerable bitterness. "It is funny what some people will do for a few francs a-month. I wonder what becomes of that kind when it goes up country?" I said to him I expected to see that soon. "So-o-o!" he exclaimed. He shuffled athwart, keeping one eye ahead vigilantly. "Don't be too sure," he continued. "The other day I took up a man who hanged himself on the road. He was a Swede, too." "Hanged himself! Why, in God's name?" I cried. He kept on looking out watchfully. "Who knows? The sun too much for him, or the country perhaps."

'At last we turned a bend. A rocky cliff appeared, mounds of turned-up earth by the shore, houses on a hill, others, with iron roofs, amongst a waste of excavations, or hanging to the declivity. A continuous noise of the rapids above hovered over this scene of inhabited devastation. A lot of people, mostly black and naked, moved about like ants. A jetty projected into the river. A blinding sunlight drowned all this at times in a sudden recrudescence of glare. "There's your Company's station," said the Swede, pointing to three wooden barrack-like structures on the rocky slope. "I will send your things up. Four boxes did you say? So. Farewell."

'I came upon a boiler wallowing in the grass, then found a path leading up the hill. It turned aside for the boulders, and also for an undersized railway-truck lying there on its back with its wheels in the air. One was off. The thing looked as dead as the carcass of some animal. I came upon more pieces of decaying machinery, a stack of rusty rails. To the left a clump of trees made a shady spot, where dark things seemed to stir feebly. I blinked, the path was steep. A horn tooted to the right, and I saw the black people run. A heavy and dull detonation shook the ground, a puff of smoke came out of the cliff, and that was all. No change appeared on the face of the rock. They were building a railway.* The cliff was not in the way or anything; but this objectless blasting was all the work going on.

'A slight clinking behind me made me turn my head. Six black men advanced in a file, toiling up the path. They walked erect and slow, balancing small baskets full of earth on their heads, and the clink kept time with their footsteps. Black rags were wound round their loins, and the short ends behind wagged to and fro like tails. I could see every rib, the joints of their limbs were like knots in a rope; each had an iron collar on his neck, and all were connected together with a chain whose bights swung between them, rhythmically clinking. Another report from the cliff made me think suddenly of that ship of war I had seen firing into a continent. It was the same kind of ominous voice; but these men could by no stretch of imagination be called enemies. They were called criminals, and the outraged law, like the bursting shells, had come to them, an insoluble mystery from over the sea. All their meagre breasts panted together, the violently dilated nostrils quivered, the eyes stared stonily up-hill. They passed me within six inches, without a glance, with that complete, deathlike indifference of unhappy savages.* Behind this raw matter one of the reclaimed, the product of the new forces at work, strolled despondently, carrying a rifle by its middle. He had a uniform jacket with a button off, and seeing a white man on the path, hoisted his weapon to his shoulder with alacrity. This was simple prudence, white men being so much alike at a distance that he could not tell who I might be. He was speedily reassured, and with a large, white, rascally grin, and a glance at his charge, seemed to take me into partnership in his exalted trust. After all, I also was a part of the great cause of these high and just proceedings.

'Instead of going up, I turned and descended to the left. My idea was to let that chain-gang get out of sight before I climbed the hill. You know I am not particularly tender; I've had to strike and to fend off. I've had to resist and to attack sometimes – that's only one way of resisting – without counting the exact cost, according to the demands of such sort of life as I had blundered into. I've seen the devil of violence, and the devil of greed, and the devil of hot desire; but, by all the stars! these were strong, lusty, red-eyed devils, that swayed and drove men – men, I tell you. But as I stood on this hillside, I foresaw that in the blinding sunshine of that land I would become acquainted with a flabby, pretending, weak-eyed devil of a rapacious and pitiless folly. How insidious he could be, too, I was only to find out several months later and a thousand miles farther. For a moment I stood appalled, as though by a warning. Finally I descended the hill, obliquely, towards the trees I had seen.

'I avoided a vast artificial hole somebody had been digging on the slope, the purpose of which I found it impossible to divine. It wasn't a quarry or a sandpit, anyhow. It was just a hole. It might have been connected with the philanthropic desire of giving the criminals something to do. I don't know. Then I nearly fell into a very narrow ravine, almost no more than a scar in the hillside. I discovered that a lot of imported drainage-pipes for the settlement had been tumbled in there. There wasn't one that was not broken. It was a wanton smash-up. At last I got under the trees. My purpose was to stroll into the shade for a moment; but it seemed to me I had stepped into the gloomy circle of some Inferno.* The river was near, and an uninterrupted, uniform, headlong, rushing noise filled the mournful stillness of the grove, where not a breath stirred, not a leaf moved, with a mysterious sound, as though the tearing pace of the launched earth had suddenly become audible.

'Black shapes crouched, lay, sat between the trees, leaning against the trunks, clinging to the earth, half coming out, half effaced within the dim light, in all the attitudes of pain, abandonment, and despair. Another mine on the cliff went off, followed by a slight shudder of the soil under my feet. The work was going on. The work! And this was the place where some of the helpers had withdrawn to die.*

'They were dying slowly – it was very clear. They were not enemies, they were not criminals, they were nothing earthly now, –nothing but black shadows of disease and starvation, lying confusedly in the greenish gloom. Brought from all the recesses of the coast in all the legality of time contracts,* lost in uncongenial surroundings, fed on unfamiliar food, they sickened, became inefficient, and were then allowed to crawl away and rest. These moribund shapes were free as air – and nearly as thin. I began to distinguish the gleam of eyes under the trees. Then, glancing down, I saw a face near my hand. The black bones reclined at full length with one shoulder against the tree, and slowly the eyelids rose and the sunken eyes looked up at me, enormous and vacant, a kind of blind, white flicker in the depths of the orbs, which died out slowly. The man seemed young – almost a boy – but you know with them it's hard to tell. I found nothing else to do but offer him one of my good Swede's ship's biscuits I had in my pocket. The fingers closed slowly on it and held – there was no other movement and no other glance. He had tied a bit of white worsted round his neck – Why? Where did he get it? Was it a badge – an ornament – a charm – a propitiatory act? Was there any idea at all connected with it? It looked startling round his black neck, this bit of white thread from beyond the seas.

'Near the same tree two more bundles of acute angles sat with their legs drawn up. One, with his chin propped on his knees, stared at nothing, in an intolerable and appalling manner. His brother phantom rested its forehead, as if overcome with a great weariness; and all about others were scattered in every pose of contorted collapse, as in some picture of a massacre or a pestilence. While I stood horror-struck, one of these creatures rose to his hands and knees, and went off on all-fours towards the river to drink. He lapped out of his hand, then sat up in the sunlight, crossing his shins in front of him, and after a time let his woolly head fall on his breastbone.

'I didn't want any more loitering in the shade, and I made haste towards the station. When near the buildings I met a white man, in such an unexpected elegance of get-up that in the first moment I took him for a sort of vision. I saw a high starched collar, white cuffs, a light alpaca jacket, snowy trousers, a clear necktie, and varnished boots. No hat. Hair parted, brushed, oiled, under a green-lined parasol held in a big white hand. He was amazing, and had a penholder behind his ear.

'I shook hands with this miracle, and I learned he was the Company's chief accountant, and that all the book-keeping was done at this station. He had come out for a moment, he said, "to get a breath of fresh air." The expression sounded wonderfully odd, with its suggestion of sedentary desk-life. I wouldn't have mentioned the fellow to you at all, only it was from his lips that I first heard the name of the man who is so indissolubly connected with the memories of that time. Moreover, I respected the fellow. Yes; I respected his collars, his vast cuffs, his brushed hair. His appearance was certainly that of a hairdresser's dummy; but in the great demoralisation of the land he kept up his appearance. That's backbone. His starched collars and got-up shirt-fronts were achievements of character. He had been out nearly three years; and, later on, I could not help asking him how he managed to sport such linen. He had just the faintest blush, and said modestly, "I've been teaching one of the native women about the station. It was difficult. She had a distaste for the work." Thus this man had verily accomplished something. And he was devoted to his books.

'Everything in the station was in a muddle, – heads, things, buildings. Strings of dusty niggers with splay feet arrived and departed; and a stream of manufactured goods, rubbishy cottons, beads, and brass-wire set into the depths of darkness, and in return came a precious trickle of ivory.

'I had to wait in the station for ten days – an eternity. I lived in a hut in the yard. To be out of the chaos I would sometimes get into the accountant's office. It was built of horizontal planks, and so badly put together that, as he bent over his high desk, he was barred from neck to heels with narrow strips of sunlight. There was no need to open the big shutter to see. It was hot there too; big flies buzzed fiendishly, and did not sting, but stabbed. I sat generally on the floor, while, of faultless appearance (and even slightly scented), perching on a high stool, he wrote, he wrote. Sometimes he stood up for exercise. When a truckle-bed with a sick man (some invalided agent from up-country) was put in there, he exhibited a gentle annoyance. "The groans of this sick person," he said, "distract my attention. And without that it is extremely difficult to guard against clerical errors in this climate."

'One day he remarked, without lifting his head, "In the interior you will no doubt meet Mr Kurtz."* On my asking who Mr Kurtz was, he said he was a first-class agent; and seeing my disappointment at this information, he added slowly, laying down his pen, "He is a very remarkable person." Further questions elicited from him that Mr Kurtz was at present in charge of a trading post, a very important one, in the true ivory-country, at "the very bottom of there. Sends in as much ivory as all the others put together . . ." He began to write again. The sick man was too ill to groan. The flies buzzed in a great peace.

'Suddenly there was a growing murmur of voices and a great tramping of feet. A caravan had come in. A violent babble of uncouth sounds burst out on the other side of the planks. All the carriers were speaking together, and in the midst of the uproar the lamentable voice of the chief agent was heard "giving it up" tearfully for the twentieth time that day . . . He rose slowly. "What a frightful row," he said. He crossed the room gently to look at the sick man, and returning, said to me, "He does not hear." "What! Dead?" I asked, startled. "No, not yet," he answered, with great composure. Then, alluding with a toss of the head to the tumult in the station-yard, "When one has got to make correct entries, one comes to hate those savages – hate them to the death." He remained thoughtful for a moment. "When you see Mr Kurtz," he went on, "tell him from me that everything here" – he glanced at the desk – "is very satisfactory. I don't like to write to him – with those messengers of ours you never know who may get your letter – at that Central Station." He stared at me for a moment with his mild, bulging eyes. "Oh, he will go far, very far," he began again. "He will be a somebody in the Administration before long. They, above – the Council in Europe, you know – mean him to be."

'He turned to his work. The noise outside had ceased, and presently as I went out I stopped at the door. In the steady buzz of flies the homeward-bound agent was lying flushed and insensible; the other, bent over his books, was making correct entries of perfectly correct transactions; and fifty feet below the doorstep I could see the still tree-tops of the grove of death.

'Next day I left that station at last, with a caravan of sixty men, for a two-hundred-mile tramp.*

'No use telling you much about that. Paths, paths, everywhere; a stamped-in network of paths spreading over the empty land, through long grass, through burnt grass, through thickets, down and up chilly ravines, up and down stony hills ablaze with heat; and a solitude, a solitude, nobody, not a hut. The population had cleared out a long time ago. Well, if a lot of mysterious niggers armed with all kinds of fearful weapons suddenly took to travelling on the road between Deal and Gravesend, catching the yokels right and left to carry heavy loads for them, I fancy every farm and cottage thereabouts would get empty very soon. Only here the dwellings were gone too. Still I passed through several abandoned villages. There's something pathetically childish in the ruins of grass walls. Day after day, with the stamp and shuffle of sixty pair of bare feet behind me, each pair under a 60-lb. load. Camp, cook, sleep, strike camp, march. Now and then a carrier dead in harness, at rest in the long grass near the path, with an empty water-gourd and his long staff lying by his side. A great silence around and above. Perhaps on some quiet night the tremor of far-of drums, sinking, swelling, a tremor vast, faint; a sound weird, appealing, suggestive, and wild – and perhaps with as respectable a meaning as the sound of bells in a Christian country. Once a white man in an unbuttoned uniform, camping on the path with an armed escort of lank Zanzibaris,* very hospitable and festive, not to say drunk. Was looking after the upkeep of the road, he declared. Can't say I saw any road or any upkeep, unless the body of a middle-aged negro, with a bullet-hole in the forehead,* upon which I absolutely stumbled three miles farther on, may be considered as a permanent improvement. I had a white companion too, not a bad chap, but rather too fleshy and with the exasperating habit of fainting on the hot hillsides, miles away from the least bit of shade and water. Annoying, you know, to hold your own coat like a parasol over a man's head while he is coming-to. I couldn't help asking him once what he meant by coming there at all. "To make money, of course. What do you think?" he said, scornfully. Then he got fever, and had to be carried in a hammock slung on a pole. As he weighed sixteen stone I had no end of rows with the carriers.* They jibbed, ran away, sneaked off with their loads in the night – quite a mutiny. So, one evening, I made a speech in English with gestures, not one of which was lost to the sixty pairs of eyes before me, and the next morning I started the hammock off in front all right. An hour afterwards I came upon the whole concern wrecked in a bush – man, hammock, groans, blankets, horrors. The heavy pole had skinned his poor nose. He was very anxious for me to kill somebody, but there wasn't the shadow of a carrier near. I remembered the old doctor, – "It would be interesting for science to watch the mental changes of individuals, on the spot." I felt I was becoming scientifically interesting. However, all that is to no purpose. On the fifteenth day I came in sight of the big river again, and hobbled into the Central Station. It was on a back water surrounded by scrub and forest, with a pretty border of smelly mud on one side, and on the three others enclosed by a crazy fence of rushes. A neglected gap was all the gate it had, and the first glance at the place was enough to let you see the flabby devil was running that show. White men with long staves in their hands appeared languidly from amongst the buildings, strolling up to take a look at me, and then retired out of sight somewhere. One of them, a stout, excitable chap with black moustaches, informed me with great volubility and many digressions, as soon as I told him who I was, that my steamer was at the bottom of the river. I was thunderstruck. What, how, why? Oh, it was "all right". The "manager himself" was there. All quite correct. "Everybody had behaved splendidly! splendidly!" – "you must," he said in agitation, "go and see the general manager at once. He is waiting!"

'I did not see the real significance of that wreck at once.* I fancy I see it now, but I am not sure – not at all. Certainly the affair was too stupid – when I think of it – to be altogether natural. Still . . . at the moment it presented itself simply as a confounded nuisance. The steamer was sunk. They had started two days before in a sudden hurry up the river with the manager on board, in charge of some volunteer skipper, and before they had been out three hours they tore the bottom out of her on stones, and she sank near the south bank. I asked myself what I was to do there, now my boat was lost. As a matter of fact, I had plenty to do in fishing my command out of the river. I had to set about it the very next day. That, and the repairs when I brought the pieces to the station, took some months.

'My first interview with the manager was curious. He did not ask me to sit down after my twenty-mile walk that morning. He was commonplace in complexion, in feature, in manners, and in voice. He was of middle size and of ordinary build. His eyes, of the usual blue, were perhaps remarkably cold, and he certainly could make his glance fall on one as trenchant and heavy as an axe. But even at these times the rest of his person seemed to disclaim the intention. Otherwise there was only an indefinable faint expression of his lips, something stealthy — a smile — not a smile — I remember it, but I can't explain. It was unconscious, this smile was, though just after he had said something it got intensified for an instant. It came at the end of his speeches like a seal applied on the words to make the meaning of the commonest phrase appear absolutely inscrutable. He was a common trader, from his youth up, employed in these parts — nothing more. He was obeyed, yet he inspired neither love nor fear, nor even respect.* He inspired uneasiness. That was it! Uneasiness. Not a definite mistrust — just uneasiness — nothing more. You have no idea how effective such a . . . a . . . faculty can be. He had no genius for organising, for initiative, or for order even. That was evident in such things as the deplorable state of the station. He had no learning, no intelligence. His position had come to him — why? Perhaps because he was never ill . . . He had served three terms of three years out there . . . Because triumphant health in the general rout of constitutions is a kind of power in itself. When he went home on leave he rioted on a large scale — pompously. Jack ashore — with a difference — in externals only. This one could gather from his casual talk. He originated nothing, he could keep the routine going — that's all. But he was great. He was great by this little thing that it was impossible to tell what could control such a man. He never gave that secret away. Perhaps there was nothing within him. Such a suspicion made one pause — for out there there were no external checks. Once when various tropical diseases had laid low almost every "agent" in the station, he was heard to say, "Men who come out here should have no entrails."* He sealed the utterance with that smile of his, as though it had been a door opening into a darkness he had in his keeping. You fancied you had seen things – but the seal was on. When annoyed at meal-times by the constant quarrels of the white men about precedence, he ordered an immense round table to be made, for which a special house had to be built. This was the station's mess-room. Where he sat was the first place – the rest were nowhere. One felt this to be his unalterable conviction. He was neither civil nor uncivil. He was quiet. He allowed his "boy" – an over-fed young negro from the coast – to treat the white men, under his very eyes, with provoking insolence.

'He began to speak as soon as he saw me. I had been very long on the road. He could not wait. Had to start without me. The up-river stations had to be relieved. There had been so many delays already that he did not know who was dead and who was alive, and how they got on – and so on, and so on. He paid no attention to my explanations, and, playing with a stick of sealing-wax, repeated several times that the situation was "very grave, very grave". There were rumours that a very important station was in jeopardy, and its chief, Mr Kurtz, was ill. Hoped it was not true. Mr Kurtz was ... I felt weary and irritable. Hang Kurtz, I thought. I interrupted him by saying I had heard of Mr Kurtz on the coast. "Ah! So they talk of him down there," he murmured to himself. Then he began again, assuring me Mr Kurtz was the best agent he had, an exceptional man, of the greatest importance to the Company; therefore I could understand his anxiety. He was, he said, "very, very uneasy". Certainly he fidgeted on his chair a good deal, exclaimed, "Ah, Mr Kurtz!" broke the stick of sealing-wax and seemed dumbfounded by the accident. Next thing he wanted to know "how long it would take to" ... I interrupted him again. Being hungry, you know, and kept on my feet too, I was getting savage. "How could I tell," I said. "I hadn't even seen the wreck yet – some months, no doubt." All this talk seemed to me so futile. "Some months," he said. "Well, let us say three months before we can make a start. Yes. That ought to do the affair." I flung out of his hut (he lived all alone in a clay hut with a sort of verandah) muttering to myself my opinion of him. He was a chattering idiot. Afterwards I took it back when it was borne in upon me startlingly with what extreme nicety he had estimated the time requisite for the "affair".

'I went to work the next day, turning, so to speak, my back on that station. In that way only it seemed to me I could keep my hold on the redeeming facts of life. Still, one must look about sometimes; and then I saw this station, these men strolling aimlessly about in the sunshine of the yard. I asked myself sometimes what it all meant? They wandered here and there with their absurd long staves in their hands, like a lot of faithless pilgrims bewitched inside a fence. The word "ivory" rang in the air, was whispered, was sighed. You would think they were praying to it. A taint of imbecile rapacity blew through it all, like a whiff from some corpse. By Jove! I've never seen anything so unreal in my life. And outside, the silent wilderness surrounding this cleared speck on the earth struck me as something great and invincible, like evil or truth, waiting patiently for the passing away of this fantastic invasion.

'Oh, these months! Well, never mind. Various things happened. One evening a grass shed full of calico, cotton prints, beads, and I don't know what else, burst into a blaze so suddenly that you would have thought the earth had opened to let an avenging fire consume all that trash. I was smoking my pipe quietly by my dismantled steamer, and saw them all cutting capers in the light, with their arms lifted high, when the stout man with moustaches came tearing down to the river, a tin pail in his hand, assured me that everybody was "behaving splendidly, splendidly", dipped about a quart of water and tore back again. I noticed there was a hole in the bottom of his pail.

'I strolled up. There was no hurry. You see the thing had gone off like a box of matches. It had been hopeless from the very first. The flame had leaped high, driven everybody back, lighted up everything — and collapsed. The shed was already a heap of embers glowing fiercely. A nigger was being beaten near by. They said he had caused the fire in some way; be that as it may, he was screeching most horribly. I saw him, later on, for several days, sitting in a bit of shade looking very sick and trying to recover himself: afterwards he arose and went out — and the wilderness without a sound took him into its bosom again. As I approached the glow from the dark I found myself at the back of two men, talking. I heard the name of Kurtz pronounced, then the words, "take advantage of this unfortunate accident".* One of the men was the manager. I wished him good evening. "Did you ever see anything like it — eh?" he said; "it is incredible," and walked off. The other man remained. He was a first-class agent, young, gentlemanly, a bit reserved, with a forked little beard and a hooked nose. He was stand-offish with the other agents. They on their side said he was the manager's spy upon them. As to me, I had hardly ever spoken to him before. We got into talk, and by-and-by we strolled away from the hissing ruins. Then he asked me to his room, which was in the main building of the station. He struck a match, and I perceived that this young aristocrat had not only a silver-mounted dressing-case but also a whole candle all to himself. Just at that time the manager was the only man supposed to have any right to candles. Native mats covered the clay walls; a collection of spears, assegais, shields, knives was hung up in trophies. The business intrusted to this fellow was the making of bricks — so I had been informed; but there wasn't a fragment of a brick anywhere in the station, and he had been there more than a year — waiting. It seems he could not make bricks without something, I don't know what — straw maybe.* Anyways, it could not be found there, and as it was not likely to be sent from Europe, it did not appear clear to me what he was waiting for. An act of special creation perhaps.* However, they were all waiting — all the sixteen or twenty pilgrims of them — for something; and upon my word it did not seem an uncongenial occupation, from the way they took it, though the only thing that ever came to them was disease — as far as I could see. They beguiled the time by backbiting and intriguing against each other in a foolish kind of way. There was an air of plotting about that station, but nothing came of it, of course. It was as unreal as everything else — as the philanthropic pretence of the whole concern, as their talk, as their government, as their show of work. The only real feeling was a desire to get appointed to a trading-post where ivory was to be had, so that they could earn percentages.* They intrigued and slandered and hated each other only on that account, – but as to effectually lifting a little finger – oh, no. By heavens! there is something after all in the world allowing one man to steal a horse while another must not look at a halter.* Steal a horse straight out. Very well. He has done it. Perhaps he can ride. Beastly, perhaps – yet still effective. But there is a way of looking at a halter that would provoke the most charitable of saints into a kick.

'I had no idea why he wanted to be sociable, but as we chatted in there it suddenly occurred to me the fellow was trying to get at something – in fact, pumping me. He alluded constantly to Europe, to the people I was supposed to know there – putting leading questions as to my acquaintances in the sepulchral city, and so on. His little eyes glittered like mica discs with curiosity, though he tried to keep up a bit of superciliousness. At first I was astonished, but very soon I became also awfully curious to see what he would find out from me. I couldn't possibly imagine what I had in me to make it worth his while. His allusions were Chinese to me.* It was very pretty to see how he baffled himself, for in truth my body was full of chills, and my head had nothing in it but that wretched steamboat business. It was evident he took me for a perfectly shameless prevaricator. At last he got angry, and, to conceal a movement of furious annoyance, he yawned. I rose. Then I noticed a small sketch in oils, on a panel, representing a woman, draped and blindfolded, carrying a lighted torch.* The background was sombre – almost black. The movement of the woman was stately, and the effect of the torchlight on the face was sinister.

'It arrested me, and he stood by, civilly holding a half-pint bottle of champagne (medical comforts) with the candle stuck in it. To my question he said Mr Kurtz had painted this – in this very station more than a year ago – while waiting for means to go to his trading-post. "Tell me, pray," said I, "who is this Mr Kurtz?"

' "The chief of the Inner Station," he answered in a short tone, looking away. "Much obliged," I said, laughing. "And you are the brickmaker of the Central Station. Every one knows that." He was silent for a while. "He is a prodigy," he said at last. "He is an emissary of pity, and science, and progress, and devil knows what else.* We want," he began to declaim suddenly, "for the guidance of the cause intrusted to us by Europe, so to speak, higher intelligence, wide sympathies, a singleness of purpose." "Who says that?" I asked. "Lots of them," he replied. "Some even write that; and so *he* comes here, a special being, as you ought to know." "Why ought I to know?" I interrupted, really surprised. He paid no attention. "Yes. To-day he is chief of the best station, next year he will be assistant-manager, two years more and . . . but I daresay you know what he will be in two years' time. You are of the new gang – the gang of virtue. The same people who sent him specially also recommended you. Oh, don't say no. I've my own eyes to trust." Light dawned upon me. My dear aunt's influential acquaintances were producing an unexpected effect upon that young man. I nearly burst into a laugh. "Do you read the Company's confidential correspondence?" I asked. He hadn't a word to say. It was great fun. "When Mr Kurtz," I continued severely, "is General Manager, you won't have the opportunity."

'He blew the candle out suddenly, and we went outside. The moon had risen. Black figures strolled about listlessly, pouring water on the glow, whence proceeded a sound of hissing. Steam ascended in the moonlight; the beaten nigger groaned somewhere. "What a row the brute makes!" said the indefatigable man with the moustaches, appearing near us. "Serve him right. Transgression – punishment – bang! Pitiless, pitiless. That's the only way. This will prevent all future conflagrations. I was just telling the manager . . ." He noticed my companion, and became crestfallen all at once. "Not in bed yet," he said, with a kind of obsequious heartiness; "it's so natural. Ha! Danger – agitation." He vanished. I went on to the river-side, and the other followed me. I heard a scathing murmur at my ear, "Heap of muffs – go to." The pilgrims could be seen in knots gesticulating, discussing. Several had still their staves in their hands. I verily believe they took these sticks to bed with them. Beyond the fence the forest stood up spectrally in the moonlight, and through the dim stir, through the faint sounds of that lamentable courtyard, the silence of the land went home to one's very heart, – its mystery, its greatness, the amazing reality of its concealed life. The hurt nigger moaned feebly somewhere near by, and then fetched a deep sigh that made me mend my pace away from there. I felt a hand introducing itself under my arm. "My dear sir," said the fellow, "I don't want to be misunderstood, and especially by you, who will see Mr Kurtz long before I can have that pleasure. I wouldn't like him to get a false idea of my disposition . . ."

'I let him run on, this papier-mâché Mephistopheles,* and it seemed to me that if I tried I could poke my forefinger through him, and find nothing inside but a little loose dirt, maybe. He, don't you see, had been planning to be assistant-manager by-and-by under the present man, and I could see that the coming of that Kurtz had upset them both not a little. He talked precipitately, and I did not try to stop him. I had my shoulders against the wreck of my steamer, hauled up on the slope like a carcass of some big river animal. The smell of mud, of primeval mud, by Jove! was in my nostrils, the high stillness of primeval forest was before my eyes; there were shiny patches on the black creek. The moon had spread over everything a thin layer of silver – over the rank grass, over the mud, upon the wall of matted vegetation standing higher than the wall of a temple, over the great river I could see through a sombre gap glittering, glittering, as it flowed broadly by without a murmur. All this was great, expectant, mute, while the man jabbered about himself. I wondered whether the stillness on the face of the immensity looking at us two were meant as an appeal or as a menace. What were we who had strayed in here? Could we handle that dumb thing, or would it handle us? I felt how big, how confoundedly big, was that thing that couldn't talk, and perhaps was deaf as well. What was in there? I could see a little ivory coming out from there, and I had heard Mr Kurtz was in there. I had heard enough about it too – God knows! Yet somehow it didn't bring any image with it – no more than if I had been told an angel or a fiend was in there. I believed it in the same way one of you might believe there are inhabitants in the planet Mars. I knew once a Scotch sailmaker who was certain, dead sure, there were people in Mars. If you asked him for some idea how they looked and behaved, he would get shy and mutter something about "walking on all-fours". If you as much as smiled, he would – though a man of sixty – offer to fight you. I would not have gone so far as to fight for Kurtz, but I went for him near enough to a lie. You know I hate, detest, and can't bear a lie, not because I am straighter than the rest of us, but simply because it appals me. There is a taint of death, a flavour of mortality in lies, – which is exactly what I hate and detest in the world – what I want to forget. It makes me miserable and sick, like biting something rotten would do. Temperament, I suppose. Well, I went near enough to it by letting the young fool there believe anything he liked to imagine as to my influence in Europe. I became in an instant as much of a pretence as the rest of the bewitched pilgrims. This simply because I had a notion it somehow would be of help to that Kurtz whom at the time I did not see – you understand. He was just a word for me. I did not see the man in the name any more than you do. Do you see him? Do you see the story? Do you see anything? It seems to me I am trying to tell you a dream – making a vain attempt, because no relation of a dream can convey the dream-sensation, that commingling of absurdity, surprise, and bewilderment in a tremor of struggling revolt, that notion of being captured by the incredible which is of the very essence of dreams . . .'

He was silent for a while.

'. . . No, it is impossible; it is impossible to convey the life-sensation of any given epoch of one's existence, – that which makes its truth, its meaning – its subtle and penetrating essence. It is impossible. We live, as we dream – alone . . .'*

He paused again as if reflecting, then added —

'Of course in this you fellows see more than I could then. You see me, whom you know . . .'

It had become so pitch dark that we listeners could hardly see one another. For a long time already he, sitting apart, had been no more to us than a voice. There was not a word from anybody. The others might have been asleep, but I was awake. I listened, I listened on the watch for the sentence, for the word, that would give me the clue to the faint uneasiness inspired by this narrative that seemed to shape itself without human lips in the heavy night-air of the river.

'. . . Yes — I let him run on,' Marlow began again, 'and think what he pleased about the powers that were behind me. I did! And there was nothing behind me! There was nothing but that wretched, old, mangled steamboat I was leaning against, while he talked fluently about "the necessity for every man to get on". "And when one comes out here, you conceive, it is not to gaze at the moon." Mr Kurtz was a "universal genius", but even a genius would find it easier to work with "adequate tools — intelligent men". He did not make bricks — why, there was a physical impossibility in the way — as I was well aware; and if he did secretarial work for the manager, it was because "no sensible man rejects wantonly the confidence of his superiors". Did I see it? I saw it. What more did I want? What I really wanted was rivets, by heaven! Rivets. To get on with the work — to stop the hole. Rivets I wanted. There were cases of them down at the coast — cases — piled up — burst — split! You kicked a loose rivet at every second step in that station yard on the hillside. Rivets had rolled into the grove of death. You could fill your pockets with rivets for the trouble of stooping down — and there wasn't one rivet to be found where it was wanted. We had plates that would do, but nothing to fasten them with. And every week the messenger, a lone negro, letter-bag on shoulder and staff in hand, left our station for the coast. And several times a week a coast caravan came in with trade goods, — ghastly glazed calico that made you shudder only to look at it, glass beads value about a penny a quart, confounded spotted cotton handkerchiefs. And no rivets. Three carriers could have brought all that was wanted to set that steamboat afloat.

'He was becoming confidential now, but I fancy my unresponsive attitude must have exasperated him at last, for he judged it necessary to inform me he feared neither God nor devil, let alone any mere man. I said I could see that very well, but what I wanted was a certain quantity of rivets — and rivets were what really Mr Kurtz wanted, if he had only known it. Now letters went to the coast every week. . . . "My dear sir," he cried, "I write from dictation." I demanded rivets. There was a way – for an intelligent man. He changed his manner; became very cold, and suddenly began to talk about a hippopotamus;* wondered whether sleeping in the steamer (I stuck to my salvage night and day) I wasn't disturbed. There was an old hippo that had the bad habit of getting out on the bank and roaming at night over the station grounds. The pilgrims used to turn out in a body and empty every rifle they could lay hands on at him. Some even had sat up o' nights for him. All this energy was wasted, though. "That animal has a charmed life," he said; "but you can say this only of brutes in this country. No man – you apprehend me? – no man here bears a charmed life." He stood there for a moment in the moonlight with his delicate hooked nose set a little askew, and his mica eyes glitering without a wink. Then, with a curt good-night, he strode off. I could see he was disturbed and considerably puzzled, which made me feel more hopeful than I had been for days. It was a great comfort to turn from that chap to my influential friend, the battered, twisted, ruined, tin-pot steamboat. I clambered on board. She rang under my feet like an empty Huntley and Palmer biscuit-tin kicked along a gutter; she was nothing so solid in make, and rather less pretty in shape, but I had expended enough hard work on her to make me love her. No influential friend would have served me better. She had given me a chance to come out a bit – to find out what I could do. No, I don't like work. I had rather laze about and think of all the fine things that can be done. I don't like work – no man does – but I like what is in the work, – the chance to find yourself. Your own reality – for yourself, not for others – what no other man can ever know. They can only see the mere show, and never can tell what it really means.

'I was not surprised to see somebody sitting aft, on the deck, with his legs dangling over the mud. You see I rather chummed with the few mechanics there were in that station, whom the other pilgrims naturally despised – on account of their imperfect manners, I suppose. This was the foreman – a boiler-maker by trade – a good worker. He was a lank, bony, yellow-faced man, with big intense eyes. His aspect was worried, and his head was as bald as the palm of my hand; but his hair in falling seemed to have stuck to his chin, and had prospered in the new locality, for his beard hung down to his waist. He was a widower with six young children (he had left them in charge of a sister of his to come out there), and the passion of his life was pigeon-flying. He was an enthusiast and a connoisseur. He raved about pigeons. After work hours he used sometimes to come over from his hut for a talk about his children and his pigeons. At work, when he had to crawl in the mud under the bottom of the steamboat, he would tie up that beard of his in a kind of white serviette he brought for the purpose. It had loops to go over his ears. In the evening he could be seen squatted on the bank rinsing that wrapper in the creek with great care, then spreading it solemnly on a bush to dry.

'I slapped him on the back and shouted "We shall have rivets!" He scrambled to his feet exclaiming "No! Rivets!" as though he couldn't believe his ears. Then in a low voice, "You . . . eh?" I don't know why we behaved like lunatics. I put my finger to the side of my nose and nodded mysteriously. "Good for you!" he cried, snapped his fingers above his head, lifting one foot. I tried a jig. We capered on the iron deck. A frightful clatter came out of that hulk, and the virgin forest on the other bank of the creek sent it back in a thundering roll upon the sleeping station. It must have made some of the pilgrims sit up in their hovels. A dark figure obscured the lighted doorway of the manager's hut, vanished, then, a second or so after, the doorway itself vanished too. We stopped, and the silence driven away by the stamping of our feet flowed back again from the recesses of the land. The great wall of vegetation, an exuberant and entangled mass of trunks, branches, leaves, boughs, festoons, motionless in the moonlight, was like a rioting invasion of soundless life, a rolling wave of plants, piled up, crested, ready to topple over the creek, to sweep every little man of us out of his little existence. And it moved not. A deadened burst of mighty splashes and snorts reached us from afar, as though an ichthyosaurus had been taking a bath of glitter in the great river. "After all," said the boilermaker in a reasonable tone, "why shouldn't we get the rivets." Why not, indeed! I did not know of any reason why we shouldn't. "They'll come in three weeks," I said, confidently.

'But they didn't. Instead came an invasion, an infliction, a visitation. It came in sections during the next three weeks, each section headed by a donkey carrying a white man in new clothes and tan shoes, bowing from that elevation right and left to the impressed pilgrims. A quarrelsome band of footsore sulky niggers trod on the heels of the donkey. A lot of tents, camp-stools, tin boxes, white cases, brown bales would be shot down in the courtyard, and the air of mystery would deepen a little over the muddle of the station. Five such instalments came, with their absurd air of disorderly flight with the loot of innumerable outfit shops and provision stores, that, one would think, they were lugging, after a raid, into the wilderness for equitable division. It was an inextricable mess of things decent in themselves but that human folly made look like the spoils of thieving.

'This devoted band called itself the Eldorado Expedition, and I believe they were sworn to secrecy. Their talk, however, was the talk of sordid buccaneers. It was reckless without hardihood, greedy without audacity, and cruel without courage. There was not an atom of foresight or of serious intention in the whole batch of them, and they did not seem aware these things are wanted for the work of the world. Their desire was to tear treasure out of the bowels of the land with no more moral purpose at the back of it than there is in burglars breaking into a safe. Who paid for the noble enterprise I don't know; but the uncle of our manager was leader of that lot.*

'In exterior he resembled a butcher in a poor neighbourhood, and his eyes had a look of sleepy cunning. He carried his fat paunch with ostentation on his short legs, and all the time his gang infested the station spoke to no one but his nephew. You could see these two roaming about all day long with their heads close together in an everlasting confab.

'I had given up worrying myself about the rivets. One's capacity for that kind of folly is more limited than you would suppose. I said Hang! – and let things slide. I had plenty of time for meditation, and now and then I would give some thought to Kurtz. I wasn't very curious about him. No. Still, I was curious to see whether this man, who had come out equipped with moral ideas of some sort, would climb to the top after all, and how he would set about his work when there.'

PART II

'One evening as I was lying flat on the deck of my steam-boat, I heard voices approaching – and there was the nephew and the uncle strolling along the bank. I laid my head on my arm again, and had nearly lost myself in a doze, when somebody said in my ear, as it were: "I am as harmless as a little child, but I don't like to be dictated to. Am I the manager – or am I not? I was ordered to send him there. It's incredible." . . . I became aware that the two were standing on the shore alongside the forepart of the steamboat, just below my head. I did not move; it did not occur to me to move. I was sleepy. "It *is* unpleasant," grunted the uncle. "He has asked the Administration to be sent there," said the other, "with the idea of showing what he could do; and I was instructed accordingly. Look at the influence that man must have. Is it not frightful?" They both agreed it was frightful, then made several bizarre remarks: "Make rain and fine weather – one man – the Council – by the nose" – bits of absurd sentences that got the better of my drowsiness, so that I had pretty near the whole of my wits about me when the uncle said, "The climate may do away with this difficulty for you. Is he alone there?" "Yes," answered the manager; "he sent his assistant down the river with a note to me in these terms: 'Clear this poor devil out of the country, and don't bother sending more of that sort. I had rather be alone than have the kind of men you can dispose of with me.' It was more than a year ago. Can you imagine such impudence!" "Anything since then?" asked the other, hoarsely. "Ivory," jerked the nephew; "lots of it – prime sort – lots – most annoying, from him." "And with that?" questioned the heavy rumble. "Invoice," was the reply fired out, so to speak. Then silence. They had been talking about Kurtz.

'I was broad awake by this time, but, lying perfectly at ease, remained still, having no inducement to change my position. "How did that ivory come all this way?" growled the elder man, who seemed very vexed. The other explained that it had come with a fleet of canoes in charge of an English half-caste clerk Kurtz had with him; that Kurtz had apparently intended to return himself, the station being by that time bare of goods and stores, but after coming three hundred miles, had suddenly decided to go back, which he started to do alone in a small dug-out with four paddlers, leaving the half-caste to continue down the river with the ivory. The two fellows there seemed astounded at anybody attempting such a thing. They were at a loss for an adequate motive. As to me, I seemed to see Kurtz for the first time. It was a distinct glimpse. The dug-out, four paddling savages, and the lone white man turning his back suddenly on the headquarters, on relief, on thoughts of home – perhaps; setting his face towards the depths of the wilderness, towards his empty and desolate station. I did not know the motive. Perhaps he was just simply a fine fellow who stuck to his work for its own sake. His name, you understand, had not been pronounced once. He was "that man". The half-caste, who, as far as I could see, had conducted a difficult trip with great prudence and pluck, was invariably alluded to as "that scoundrel". The "scoundrel" had said the "man" had been ill – had recovered . . . The two below me moved away then a few paces, and strolled back and forth at some little distance. I heard: "Military post – doctor – two hundred miles – quite alone now – unavoidable delays – nine months – no news – strange rumours." They approached again, just as the manager was saying, "Nobody unless a species of wandering trader – a pestilential fellow, snapping ivory from the natives." Who was it they were talking about now? I gathered in snatches that this was some man supposed to be in Kurtz's district, and of whom the manager did not approve. "We will not be free from unfair competition till one of these fellows is hanged for an example," he said. "Certainly," grunted the other; "get him hanged! Why not?* Anything – anything can be done in this country. That's what I say; nobody here, you understand, *here*, can endanger your position. And why? You stand the climate – you outlast them all. The danger is in Europe; but there before I left I took care to —" They moved off and whispered, then their voices rose again. 'The extraordinary series of delays is not my fault. I did my possible." The fat man sighed, "Very sad." "And the pestiferous absurdity of his talk," continued the other; "he bothered me enough when he was here. 'Each station should be like a beacon on the road towards better things, a centre for trade of course, but also for humanising, improving, instructing.' Conceive you – that ass!* And he wants to be manager! No, it's —" Here he got choked by excessive indignation, and I lifted my head the least bit. I was surprised to see how near they were – right under me. I could have spat upon their hats. They were looking on the ground, absorbed in thought. The manager was switching his leg with a slender twig: his sagacious relative lifted his head. "You have been well since you came out this time?" he asked. The other gave a start. "Who? I? Oh! Like a charm – like a charm. But the rest – oh, my goodness! All sick. They die so quick, too, that I haven't the time to send them out of the country – it's incredible!" "H'm. Just so," grunted the uncle. "Ah! my boy, trust to this – I say, trust to this." I saw him extend his short flipper of an arm for a semicircular gesture that took in the forest, the creek, the mud, the river, – seemed to beckon with a dishonouring flourish before the sunlit face of the land a treacherous appeal to the lurking death, to the hidden evil, to the profound darkness of its heart. It was so startling that I leaped to my feet and looked back at the edge of the forest, as though I had expected an answer of some sort to that black display of confidence. You know the foolish notions that come to one sometimes. The high stillness confronted these two figures with its ominous patience, waiting for the passing away of a fantastic invasion.

'They swore aloud together – out of sheer fright, I believe – then pretending not to know anything of my existence, turned back to the station. The sun was low; and leaning forward side by side, they seemed to be tugging painfully uphill their two ridiculous shadows of unequal length, that trailed behind them slowly over the tall grass without bending a single blade.

'In a few days the Eldorado Expedition went into the patient wilderness, that closed upon them as the sea closes over a diver. Long afterwards the news came that all the donkeys were dead. I know nothing as to the fate of the less valuable animals.* They, no doubt, like the rest of us, found what they deserved. I did not inquire. I was then rather excited at the prospect of meeting Kurtz very soon. When I say very soon I mean comparatively. It was just two months from the day we left the creek when we came to the bank below Kurtz's station.

'Going up that river was like travelling back to the earliest beginnings of the world, when vegetation rioted on the earth and the big trees were kings. An empty stream, a great silence, an impenetrable forest. The air was warm, thick, heavy, sluggish. There was no joy in the brilliance of sunshine. The long stretches of the waterway ran on, deserted, into the gloom of over-shadowed distances. On silvery sandbanks hippos and alligators* sunned themselves side by side. The broadening waters flowed through a mob of wooded islands; you lost your way on that river as you would in a desert, and butted all day long against shoals, trying to find the channel, till you thought yourself bewitched and cut off for ever from everything you had known once – somewhere – far away – in another existence perhaps. There were moments when one's past came back to one, as it will sometimes when you have not a moment to spare to yourself; but it came in the shape of an unrestful and noisy dream, remembered with wonder amongst the overwhelming realities of this strange world of plants, and water, and silence. And this stillness of life did not in the least resemble a peace. It was the stillness of an implacable force brooding over an inscrutable intention. It looked at you with a vengeful aspect. I got used to it afterwards; I did not see it any more; I had no time. I had to keep guessing at the channel; I had to discern, mostly by inspiration, the signs of hidden banks; I watched for sunken stones; I was learning to clap my teeth smartly before my heart flew out, when I shaved by a fluke some infernal sly old snag that would have ripped the life out of the tin-pot steamboat and drowned all the pilgrims; I had to keep a look-out for the signs of dead wood we could cut up in the night for next day's steaming.* When you have to attend to things of that sort, to the mere incidents of the surface, the reality – the reality, I tell you – fades. The inner truth is hidden – luckily, luckily. But I felt it all the same; I felt often its mysterious stillness watching me at my monkey tricks, just as it watches you fellows performing on your respective tight-ropes for – what is it? half-a-crown a tumble –'

'Try to be civil, Marlow,' growled a voice, and I knew there was at least one listener awake besides myself.

'I beg your pardon. I forgot the heartache which makes up the rest of the price. And indeed what does the price matter, if the trick be well done? You do your tricks very well. And I didn't do badly either, since I managed not to sink that steamboat on my first trip. It's a wonder to me yet. Imagine a blindfolded man set to drive a van over a bad road. I sweated and shivered over that business considerably, I can tell you. After all, for a seaman, to scrape the bottom of the thing that's supposed to float all the time under his care is the unpardonable sin. No one may know of it, but you never forget the thump – eh? A blow on the very heart. You remember it, you dream of it, you wake up at night and think of it – years after – and go hot and cold all over. I don't pretend to say that steamboat floated all the time. More than once she had to wade for a bit, with twenty cannibals splashing around and pushing. We had enlisted some of these chaps on the way for a crew. Fine fellows – cannibals – in their place.* They were men one could work with, and I am grateful to them. And, after all, they did not eat each other before my face: they had brought along a provision of hippo-meat which went rotten, and made the mystery of the wilderness stink in my nostrils. Phoo! I can sniff it now. I had the manager on board and three or four pilgrims with their staves – all complete. Sometimes we came upon a station close by the bank, clinging to the skirts of the unknown, and the white men rushing out of a tumble-down hovel, with great gestures of joy and surprise and welcome, seemed very strange, – had the appearance of being held there captive by a spell. The word ivory would ring in the air for a while – and on we went again into the silence, along empty reaches, round the still bends, between the high walls of our winding way, reverberating in hollow claps the ponderous beat of the sternwheel. Trees, trees, millions of trees, massive, immense, running up high; and at their foot, hugging the bank against the stream, crept the little begrimed steamboat, like a sluggish beetle crawling on the floor of a lofty portico. It made you feel very small, very lost, and yet it was not altogether depressing that feeling. After all, if you were small, the grimy beetle crawled on – which was just what you wanted it to do. Where the pilgrims imagined it crawled to I don't know. To some place where they expected to get something, I bet! For me it crawled towards Kurtz – exclusively; but when the steam-pipes started leaking we crawled very slow. The reaches opened before us and closed behind, as if the forest had stepped leisurely across the water to bar the way for our return. We penetrated deeper and deeper into the heart of darkness. It was very quiet there. At night sometimes the roll of drums behind the curtain of trees would run up the river and remain sustained faintly, as if hovering in the air high over our heads, till the first break of day. Whether it meant war, peace, or prayer we could not tell. The dawns were heralded by the descent of a chill stillness; the wood-cutters slept, their fires burned low; the snapping of a twig would make you start. We were wanderers on a prehistoric earth, on an earth that wore the aspect of an unknown planet. We could have fancied ourselves the first of men taking possession of an accursed inheritance, to be subdued at the cost of profound anguish and of excessive toil. But suddenly, as we struggled round a bend, there would be a glimpse of rush walls, of peaked grass-roofs, a burst of yells, a whirl of black limbs, a mass of hands clapping, of feet stamping, of bodies swaying, of eyes rolling, under the droop of heavy and motionless foliage. The steamer toiled along slowly on the edge of a black and incomprehensible frenzy. The prehistoric man was cursing us, praying to us, welcoming us – who could tell? We were cut off from the comprehension of our surroundings; we glided past like phantoms, wondering and secretly appalled, as sane men would be before an enthusiastic outbreak in a madhouse. We could not understand, because we were too far and could not remember, because we were travelling in the night of first ages, of those ages that are gone, leaving hardly a sign – and no memories.

'The earth seemed unearthly. We are accustomed to look upon the shackled form of a conquered monster, but there – there you could look at a thing monstrous and free. It was unearthly, and the men were – No, they were not inhuman. Well, you know, that was the worst of it – this suspicion of their not being inhuman. It would come slowly to one. They howled, and leaped, and spun, and made horrid faces; but what thrilled you was just the thought of their humanity – like yours – the thought of your remote kinship with this wild and passionate uproar. Ugly. Yes, it was ugly enough; but if you were man enough you would admit to yourself that there was in you just the faintest trace of a response to the terrible frankness of that noise, a dim suspicion of there being a meaning in it which you – you so remote from the night of first ages – could comprehend. And why not? The mind of man is capable of anything – because everything is in it, all the past as well as all the future. What was there after all? Joy, fear, sorrow, devotion, valour, rage – who can tell? – but truth – truth stripped of its cloak of time. Let the fool gape and shudder – the man knows, and can look on without a wink. But he must at least be as much of a man as these on the shore. He must meet that truth with his own true stuff – with his own inborn strength. Principles? Principles won't do. Acquisitions, clothes, pretty rags – rags that would fly off at the first good shake.* No; you want a deliberate belief. An appeal to me in this fiendish row – is there? Very well; I hear; I admit, but I have a voice too, and for good or evil mine is the speech that cannot be silenced. Of course, a fool, what with sheer fright and fine sentiments, is always safe. Who's that grunting? You wonder I didn't go ashore for a howl and a dance? Well, no – I didn't. Fine sentiments, you say? Fine sentiments, be hanged! I had no time. I had to mess about with white-lead and strips of woollen blanket helping to put bandages on those leaky steam-pipes – I tell you. I had to watch the steering, and circumvent those snags, and get the tin-pot along by hook or by crook. There was surface-truth enough in these things to save a wiser man. And between whiles I had to look after the savage who was fireman. He was an improved specimen; he could fire up a vertical boiler. He was there below me, and, upon my word, to look at him was as edifying as seeing a dog in a parody of breeches and a feather hat, walking on his hind-legs. A few months of training had done for that really fine chap. He squinted at the steam-gauge and at the water-gauge with an evident effort of intrepidity — and he had filed teeth too, the poor devil, and the wool of his pate shaved into queer patterns, and three ornamental scars on each of his cheeks. He ought to have been clapping his hands and stamping his feet on the bank, instead of which he was hard at work, a thrall to strange witchcraft, full of improving knowledge. He was useful because he had been instructed; and what he knew was this — that should the water in that transparent thing disappear, the evil spirit inside the boiler would get angry through the greatness of his thirst, and take a terrible vengeance.* So he sweated and fired up and watched the glass fearfully (with an impromptu charm, made of rags, tied to his arm, and a piece of polished bone, as big as a watch, stuck flatways through his lower lip), while the wooded banks slipped past us slowly, the short noise was left behind, the interminable miles of silence — and we crept on, towards Kurtz. But the snags were thick, the water was treacherous and shallow, the boiler seemed indeed to have a sulky devil in it, and thus neither that fireman nor I had any time to peer into our creepy thoughts.

'Some fifty miles below the Inner Station we came upon a hut of reeds, an inclined and melancholy pole, with the unrecognisable tatters of what had been a flag of some sort flying from it, and a neatly stacked wood-pile. This was unexpected. We came to the bank, and on the stack of firewood found a flat piece of board with some faded pencil-writing on it. When deciphered it said: "Wood for you. Hurry up. Approach cautiously." There was a signature, but it was illegible — not Kurtz — a much longer word. Hurry up. Where? Up the river? "Approach cautiously." We had not done so. But the warning could not have been meant for the place where it could be only found after approach. Something was wrong above. But what — and how much? That was the question. We commented adversely upon the imbecility of that telegraphic style. The bush around said nothing, and would not let us look very far, either. A torn curtain of red twill hung in the doorway of the hut, and flapped sadly in our faces. The dwelling was dismantled; but we could see a white man had lived there not very long ago. There remained a rude table – a plank on two posts; a heap of rubbish reposed in a dark corner, and by the door I picked up a book. It had lost its covers, and the pages had been thumbed into a state of extremely dirty softness; but the back had been lovingly stitched afresh with white cotton thread, which looked clean yet. It was an extraordinary find. Its title was, "An Inquiry into some Points of Seamanship", by a man Tower, Towson – some such name – Master in his Majesty's Navy.* The matter looked dreary reading enough, with illustrative diagrams and repulsive tables of figures, and the copy was sixty years old. I handled this amazing antiquity with the greatest possible tenderness, lest it should dissolve in my hands. Within, Towson or Towser was inquiring earnestly into the breaking strain of ships' chains and tackle, and other such matters. Not a very enthralling book; but at the first glance you could see there a singleness of intention, an honest concern for the right way of going to work, which made these humble pages, thought out so many years ago, luminous with another than a professional light. The simple old sailor, with his talk of chains and purchases, made me forget the jungle and the pilgrims in a delicious sensation of having come upon something unmistakably real. Such a book being there was wonderful enough; but still more astounding were the notes pencilled in the margin, and plainly referring to the text. I couldn't believe my eyes! They were in cipher! Yes, it looked like cipher. Fancy a man lugging with him a book of that description into this nowhere and studying it – and making notes – in cipher at that! It was an extravagant mystery.

'I had been dimly aware for some time of a worrying noise, and when I lifted my eyes I saw the wood-pile was gone, and the manager, aided by all the pilgrims, was shouting at me from the river-side. I slipped the book into my pocket. I assure you to leave off reading was like tearing myself away from the shelter of an old and solid friendship.

'I started the lame engine ahead. "It must be this miserable trader – this intruder," exclaimed the manager, looking back malevolently at the place we had left. "He must be English," I said. "It will not save him from getting into trouble if he is not careful," muttered the manager darkly. I observed with assumed innocence that no man was safe from trouble in this world.

'The current was more rapid now, the steamer seemed at her last gasp, the stern-wheel flopped languidly, and I caught myself listening on tiptoe for the next beat of the float, for in sober truth I expected the wretched thing to give up every moment. It was like watching the last flickers of a life. But still we crawled. Sometimes I would pick out a tree a little way ahead to measure our progress towards Kurtz by, but I lost it invariably before we got abreast. To keep the eyes so long on one thing was too much for human patience. The manager displayed a beautiful resignation. I fretted and fumed and took to arguing with myself whether or no I would talk openly with Kurtz; but before I could come to any conclusion it occurred to me that my speech or my silence, indeed any action of mine, would be a mere futility. What did it matter what any one knew or ignored? What did it matter who was manager? One gets sometimes such a flash of insight. The essentials of this affair lay deep under the surface, beyond my reach, and beyond my power of meddling.

'Towards the evening of the second day we judged ourselves about eight miles from Kurtz's station. I wanted to push on; but the manager looked grave, and told me the navigation up there was so dangerous that it would be advisable, the sun being very low already, to wait where we were till next morning. Moreover, he pointed out that if the warning to approach cautiously were to be followed, we must approach in daylight—not at dusk, or in the dark. This was sensible enough. Eight miles meant nearly three hours' steaming for us, and I could also see suspicious ripples at the upper end of the reach. Nevertheless, I was annoyed beyond expression at the delay, and most unreasonably too, since one night more could not matter much after so many months. As we had plenty of wood, and caution was the word, I brought up in the middle of the stream. The reach was narrow, straight, with high sides like a railway cutting. The dusk came gliding into it long before the sun had set. The current ran smooth and swift, but a dumb immobility sat on the banks. The living trees, lashed together by the creepers and every living bush of the undergrowth, might have been changed into stone, even to the slenderest twig, to the lightest leaf. It was not sleep – it seemed unnatural, like a state of trance. Not the faintest sound of any kind could be heard. You looked on amazed, and began to suspect yourself of being deaf – then the night came suddenly, and struck you blind as well. About three in the morning some large fish leaped, and the loud splash made me jump as though a gun had been fired. When the sun rose there was a white fog, very warm and clammy, and more blinding than the night. It did not shift or drive; it was just there, standing all round you like something solid. At eight or nine, perhaps, it lifted as a shutter lifts. We had a glimpse of the towering multitude of trees, of the immense matted jungle, with the blazing little ball of the sun hanging over it – all perfectly still – and then the white shutter came down again, smoothly, as if sliding in greased grooves. I ordered the chain, which we had begun to heave in, to be paid out again. Before it stopped running with a muffled rattle, a cry, a very loud cry, as of infinite desolation, soared slowly in the opaque air. It ceased. A complaining clamour, modulated in savage discords, filled our ears. The sheer unexpectedness of it made my hair stir under my cap. I don't know how it struck the others: to me it seemed as though the mist itself had screamed, so suddenly, and apparently from all sides at once, did this tumultuous and mournful uproar arise. It culminated in a hurried outbreak of almost intolerably excessive shrieking, which stopped short, leaving us stiffened in a variety of silly attitudes, and obstinately listening to the nearly as appalling and excessive silence. "Good God! What is the meaning —?" stammered at my elbow one of the pilgrims, – a little fat man, with sandy hair and red whiskers, who wore side-spring boots, and pink pyjamas tucked into his socks. Two others remained open-mouthed a whole minute, then dashed into the little cabin, to rush out incontinently and stand darting scared glances, with Winchesters at "ready" in their hands. What we could see was just the steamer we were on, her outlines blurred as though she had been on the point of dissolving, and a misty strip of water, perhaps two feet broad, around her – and that was all. The rest of the world was nowhere, as far as our eyes and ears were concerned. Just nowhere. Gone, disappeared; swept off without leaving a whisper or a shadow behind.

'I went forward, and ordered the chain to be hauled in short, so as to be ready to trip the anchor and move the steamboat at once if necessary. "Will they attack?" whispered an awed voice. "We will be all butchered in this fog," murmured another. The faces twitched with the strain, the hands trembled slightly, the eyes forgot to wink. It was very curious to see the contrast of expressions of the white men and of the black fellows of our crew, who were as much strangers to that part of the river as we, though their homes were only eight hundred miles away. The whites, of course greatly discomposed, had besides a curious look of being painfully shocked by such an outrageous row. The others had an alert, naturally interested expression; but their faces were essentially quiet, even those of the one or two who grinned as they hauled at the chain. Several exchanged short, grunting phrases, which seemed to settle the matter to their satisfaction. Their headman, a young, broad-chested black, severely draped in dark-blue fringed cloths, with fierce nostrils and his hair all done up artfully in oily ringlets, stood near me. "Aha!" I said, just for good fellowship's sake. "Catch 'im," he snapped, with a bloodshot widening of his eyes and a flash of sharp teeth – "catch 'im. Give 'im to us." "To you, eh?' I asked; "what would you do with them?" "Eat 'im!" he said, curtly, and, leaning his elbow on the rail, looked out into the fog in a dignified and profoundly pensive attitude. I would no doubt have been properly horrified, had it not occurred to me that he and his chaps must be very hungry: that they must have been growing increasingly hungry for at least this month past. They had been engaged for six months (I don't think a single one of them had any clear idea of time, as we at the end of countless ages have. They still belonged to the beginnings of time – had no inherited experience to teach them as it were), and of course, as long as there was a piece of paper written over in accordance with some farcical law or other made down the river, it didn't enter anybody's head to trouble how they would live.

Certainly they had brought with them some rotten hippo-meat, which couldn't have lasted very long, anyway, even if the pilgrims hadn't, in the midst of a shocking hullabaloo, thrown a considerable quantity of it overboard. It looked like a high-handed proceeding; but it was really a case of legitimate self-defence. You can't breathe dead hippo waking, sleeping, and eating, and at the same time keep your precarious grip on existence. Besides that, they had given them every week three pieces of brass wire, each about nine inches long; and the theory was they were to buy their provisions with that currency in river-side villages.* You can see how *that* worked. There were either no villages, or the people were hostile, or the director, who like the rest of us fed out of tins, with an occasional old he-goat thrown in, didn't want to stop the steamer for some more or less recondite reason. So, unless they swallowed the wire itself, or made loops of it to snare the fishes with, I don't see what good their extravagant salary could be to them. I must say it was paid with a regularity worthy of a large and honourable trading company. For the rest, the only thing to eat – though it didn't look eatable in the least – I saw in their possession was a few lumps of some stuff like half-cooked dough,* of a dirty lavender colour, they kept wrapped in leaves, and now and then swallowed a piece of, but so small that it seemed done more for the looks of the thing than for any serious purpose of sustenance. Why in the name of all the gnawing devils of hunger they didn't go for us – they were thirty to five – and have a good tuck in for once, amazes me now when I think of it. They were big powerful men, with not much capacity to weigh the consequences, with courage, with strength, even yet, though their skins were no longer glossy and their muscles no longer hard. And I saw that something restraining, one of those human secrets that baffle probability, had come into play there. I looked at them with a swift quickening of interest – not because it occurred to me I might be eaten by them before very long, though I own to you that just then I perceived – in a new light, as it were – how unwholesome the pilgrims looked, and I hoped, yes, I positively hoped, that my aspect was not so – what shall I say? – so – unappetising: a touch of fantastic vanity which fitted well with the dream-sensation that pervaded all my days at that time. Perhaps I had a little fever too. One can't live with one's finger everlastingly on one's pulse. I had often "a little fever", or a little touch of other things – the playful paw-strokes of the wilderness, the preliminary trifling before the more serious onslaught which came in due course. Yes; I looked at them as you would on any human being, with a curiosity of their impulses, motives, capacities, weaknesses, when brought to the test of an inexorable physical necessity. Restraint! What possible restraint? Was it superstition, disgust, patience, fear – or some kind of primitive honour? No fear can stand up to hunger, no patience can wear it out, disgust simply does not exist where hunger is; and as to superstition, beliefs, and what you may call principles, they are less than chaff in a breeze. Don't you know the devilry of lingering starvation, its exasperating torment, its black thoughts, its sombre and brooding ferocity? Well, I do. It takes a man all his inborn strength to fight hunger properly. It's really easier to face bereavement, dishonour, and the perdition of one's soul – than this kind of prolonged hunger. Sad, but true. And these chaps too had no earthly reason for any kind of scruple. Restraint! I would just as soon have expected restraint from a hyena prowling amongst the corpses of a battlefield. But there was the fact facing me – the fact dazzling, to be seen, like the foam on the depths of the sea, like a ripple on an unfathomable enigma, a mystery greater – when I thought of it – than the curious, inexplicable note of desperate grief in this savage clamour that had swept by us on the river-bank, behind the blind whiteness of the fog.

'Two pilgrims were quarrelling in hurried whispers as to which bank. "Left." "No, no; how can you? Right, right, of course." "It is very serious," said the manager's voice behind me; "I would be desolated if anything should happen to Mr Kurtz before we came up." I looked at him, and had not the slightest doubt he was sincere. He was just the kind of man who would wish to preserve appearances. That was his restraint. But when he muttered something about going on at once, I did not even take the trouble to answer him. I knew, and he knew, that it was impossible. Were we to let go our hold of the bottom, we would be absolutely in the air – in space. We wouldn't be able to tell where we were going to – whether up or down stream, or across – till we fetched against one bank or the other, – and then we wouldn't know at first which it was. Of course I made no move. I had no mind for a smash-up. You couldn't imagine a more deadly place for a shipwreck. Whether drowned at once or not, we were sure to perish speedily in one way or another. "I authorise you to take all the risks," he said, after a short silence. "I refuse to take any," I said shortly; which was just the answer he expected, though its tone might have surprised him. "Well, I must defer to your judgment. You are captain," he said, with marked civility. I turned my shoulder to him in sign of my appreciation, and looked into the fog. How long would it last? It was the most hopeless look-out. The approach to this Kurtz grubbing for ivory in the wretched bush was beset by as many dangers as though he had been an enchanted princess sleeping in a fabulous castle. "Will they attack, do you think?" asked the manager, in a confidential tone.

'I did not think they would attack, for several obvious reasons. The thick fog was one. If they left the bank in their canoes they would get lost in it, as we would be if we attempted to move. Still, I had also judged the jungle of both banks quite impenetrable – and yet eyes were in it, eyes that had seen us. The riverside bushes were certainly very thick; but the undergrowth behind was evidently penetrable. However, during the short lift I had seen no canoes anywhere in the reach – certainly not abreast of the steamer. But what made the idea of attack inconceivable to me was the nature of the noise – of the cries we had heard. They had not the fierce character boding of immediate hostile intention. Unexpected, wild, and violent as they had been, they had given me an irresistible impression of sorrow. The glimpse of the steamboat had for some reason filled those savages with unrestrained grief. The danger, if any, I expounded, was from our proximity to a great human passion let loose. Even extreme grief may ultimately vent itself in violence – but more generally takes the form of apathy . . .

'You should have seen the pilgrims stare! They had no heart to grin or even to revile me; but I believe they thought me gone mad –

with fright, maybe. I delivered a regular lecture. My dear boys, it was no good bothering. Keep a look-out? Well, you may guess I watched the fog for the signs of lifting as a cat watches a mouse; but for anything else our eyes were of no more use to us than if we had been buried miles deep in a heap of cotton-wool. It felt like it too – choking, warm, stifling. Besides, all I said, though it sounded extravagant, was absolutely true to fact. What we afterwards alluded to as an attack was really an attempt at repulse. The action was very far from being aggressive – it was not even defensive, in the usual sense: it was undertaken under the stress of desperation, and in its essence was purely protective.

'It developed itself, I should say, two hours after the fog lifted, and its commencement was at a spot, roughly speaking, about a mile and a half below Kurtz's station. We had just floundered and flopped round a bend, when I saw an islet, a mere grassy hummock of bright green, in the middle of the stream. It was the only thing of the kind; but as we opened the reach more, I perceived it was the head of a long sandbank, or rather of a chain of shallow patches stretching down the middle of the river. They were discoloured, just awash, and the whole lot was seen just under the water, exactly as a man's backbone is seen running down the middle of his back under the skin. Now, as far as I did see, I could go to the right or to the left of this. I didn't know either channel, of course. The banks looked pretty well alike, the depth appeared the same; but as I had been informed the station was on the west side, I naturally headed for the western passage.

'No sooner had we fairly entered it than I became aware it was much narrower than I had supposed. To the left of us there was the long uninterrupted shoal, and to the right a high, steep bank heavily overgrown with bushes. Above the bush the trees stood in serried ranks. The twigs overhung the current thickly, and from distance to distance a large limb of some tree projected rigidly over the stream. It was then well on in the afternoon, the face of the forest was gloomy, and a broad strip of shadow had already fallen on the water. In this shadow we steamed up – very slowly, as you may imagine. I sheered her well inshore – the water being deepest near the bank, as the sounding-pole informed me.

'One of my hungry and forbearing friends was sounding in the bows just below me. This steamboat was exactly like a decked scow. On the deck there were two little teak-wood houses, with doors and windows. The boiler was in the fore-end, and the machinery right astern. Over the whole there was a light roof, supported on stanchions. The funnel projected through that roof, and in front of the funnel a small cabin built of light planks served for a pilot-house. It contained a couch, two camp-stools, a loaded Martini-Henry leaning in one corner, a tiny table, and the steering-wheel. It had a wide door in front and a broad shutter at each side. All these were always thrown open, of course. I spent my days perched up there on the extreme fore-end of that roof, before the door. At night I slept, or tried to, on the couch. An athletic black belonging to some coast tribe, and educated by my poor predecessor, was the helmsman. He sported a pair of brass earrings, wore a blue cloth wrapper from the waist to the ankles, and thought all the world of himself. He was the most unstable kind of fool I had ever seen. He steered with no end of a swagger while you were by; but if he lost sight of you, he became instantly the prey of an abject funk, and would let that cripple of a steamboat get the upper hand of him in a minute.

'I was looking down at the sounding-pole, and feeling much annoyed to see at each try a little more of it stick out of that river, when I saw my poleman give up the business suddenly, and stretch himself flat on the deck, without even taking the trouble to haul his pole in. He kept hold on it though, and it trailed in the water. At the same time the fireman, whom I could also see below me, sat down abruptly before his furnace and ducked his head. I was amazed. Then I had to look at the river mighty quick, because there was a snag in the fairway. Sticks, little sticks, were flying about – thick: they were whizzing before my nose, dropping below me, striking behind me against my pilot-house. All this time the river, the shore, the woods, were very quiet – perfectly quiet. I could only hear the heavy splashing thump of the stern-wheel and the patter of these things. We cleared the snag clumsily. Arrows, by Jove! We were being shot at! I stepped in quickly to close the shutter on the land-side. That fool-helmsman, his hands on the spokes, was lifting his knees high, stamping his feet, champing his mouth, like a reined-in horse. Confound him! And we were staggering within ten feet of the bank. I had to lean right out to swing the heavy shutter, and I saw a face amongst the leaves on the level with my own, looking at me very fierce and steady; and then suddenly, as though a veil had been removed from my eyes, I made out, deep in the tangled gloom, naked breasts, arms, legs, glaring eyes – the bush was swarming with human limbs in movement, glistening, of bronze colour. The twigs shook, swayed, and rustled, the arrows flew out of them, and then the shutter came to. "Steer her straight," I said to the helmsman. He held his head rigid, face forward; but his eyes rolled, he kept on lifting and setting down his feet gently, his mouth foamed a little. "Keep quiet!" I said in a fury. I might just as well have ordered a tree not to sway in the wind. I darted out. Below me there was a great scuffle of feet on the iron deck, exclamations; a voice screamed, "Can you turn back?" I caught sight of a V-shaped ripple on the water ahead. What? Another snag! A fusillade burst out under my feet. The pilgrims had opened with their Winchesters, and were simply squirting lead into that bush. A deuce of a lot of smoke came up and drove slowly forward. I swore at it. Now I couldn't see the ripple or the snag either. I stood in the doorway, peering, and the arrows came in swarms. They might have been poisoned, but they looked as though they wouldn't kill a cat. The bush began to howl. Our wood-cutters raised a warlike whoop; the report of a rifle just at my back deafened me. I glanced over my shoulder, and the pilot-house was yet full of noise and smoke when I made a dash at the wheel. The fool-nigger had dropped everything, to throw the shutter open and let off that Martini-Henry. He stood before the wide opening, glaring, and I yelled at him to come back, while I straightened the sudden twist out of that steamboat. There was no room to turn even if I had wanted to, the snag was somewhere very near ahead in that confounded smoke, there was no time to lose, so I just crowded her into the bank – right into the bank, where I knew the water was deep.

'We tore slowly along the overhanging bushes in a whirl of

broken twigs and flying leaves. The fusillade below stopped short, as I had foreseen it would when the squirts got empty. I threw my head back to a glinting whizz that traversed the pilot-house, in at one shutter-whole and out at the other. Looking past that mad helmsman, who was shaking the empty rifle and yelling at the shore, I saw vague forms of men running bent double, leaping, gliding, distinct, incomplete, evanescent. Something big appeared in the air before the shutter, the rifle went overboard, and the man stepped back swiftly, looked at me over his shoulder in an extraordinary, profound, familiar manner, and fell upon my feet. The side of his head hit the wheel twice, and the end of what appeared a long cane clattered round and knocked over a little camp-stool. It looked as though after wrenching that thing from somebody ashore he had lost his balance in the effort. The thin smoke had blown away, we were clear of the snag, and looking ahead I could see that in another hundred yards or so I would be free to sheer off, away from the bank; but my feet felt so very warm and wet that I had to look down. The man had rolled on his back and stared straight up at me; both his hands clutched that cane. It was the shaft of a spear that, either thrown or lunged through the opening, had caught him in the side just below the ribs; the blade had gone in out of sight, after making a frightful gash; my shoes were full; a pool of blood lay very still, gleaming dark-red under the wheel; his eyes shone with an amazing lustre. The fusillade burst out again. He looked at me anxiously, gripping the spear like something precious, with an air of being afraid I would try to take it away from him. I had to make an effort to free my eyes from his gaze and attend to the steering. With one hand I felt above my head for the line of the steam-whistle, and jerked out screech after screech hurriedly.* The tumult of angry and warlike yells was checked instantly, and then from the depths of the woods went out such a tremulous and prolonged wail of mournful fear and utter despair as may be imagined to follow the flight of the last hope from the earth. There was a great commotion in the bush; the shower of arrows stopped, a few dropping shots rang out sharply — then silence, in which the languid beat of the stern-wheel came plainly to my ears.

I put the helm hard a-starboard at the moment when the pilgrim in pink pyjamas, very hot and agitated, appeared in the doorway. "The manager sends me —" he began in an official tone, and stopped short. "Good God!" he said, glaring at the wounded man.

'We two whites stood over him, and his lustrous and inquiring glance enveloped us both. I declare it looked as though he would presently put to us some question in an understandable language; but he died without uttering a sound, without moving a limb, without twitching a muscle. Only in the very last moment, as though in response to some sign we could not see, to some whisper we could not hear, he frowned heavily, and that frown gave to his black death-mask an inconceivably sombre, brooding, and menacing expression. The lustre of inquiring glance faded swiftly into vacant glassiness. "Can you steer?" I asked the agent eagerly. He looked very dubious; but I made a grab at his arm, and he understood at once I meant him to steer whether or no. To tell you the truth, I was morbidly anxious to change my shoes and socks. "He is dead," murmured the fellow, immensely impressed. "No doubt about it," said I, tugging like mad at the shoe-laces. "And, by the way, I suppose Mr Kurtz is dead as well by this time."

'For the moment that was the dominant thought. There was a sense of extreme disappointment, as though I had found out I had been striving after something altogether without a substance. I couldn't have been more disgusted if I had travelled all this way for the sole purpose of talking with Mr Kurtz. Talking with . . . I flung one shoe overboard, and became aware that that was exactly what I had been looking forward to – a talk with Kurtz. I made the strange discovery that I had never imagined him as doing, you know, but as discoursing. I didn't say to myself, "Now I will never see him," or "Now I will never shake him by the hand," but "Now I will never hear him." The man presented himself as a voice. Not of course that I did not connect him with some sort of action. Hadn't I been told in all the tones of jealousy and admiration that he had collected, bartered, swindled, or stolen more ivory than all the other agents together. That was not the point. The point was in his being a gifted creature, and that of all his gifts the one that stood out pre-eminently, that carried with it a sense of real presence, was his ability to talk, his words – the gift of expression, the bewildering, the illuminating, the most exalted and the most contemptible, the pulsating stream of light, or the deceitful flow from the heart of an impenetrable darkness.

'The other shoe went flying unto the devil-god of that river. I thought, By Jove! it's all over. We are too late; he has vanished – the gift has vanished, by means of some spear, arrow, or club. I will never hear that chap speak after all, – and my sorrow had a startling extravagance of emotion, even such as I had noticed in the howling sorrow of these savages in the bush. I couldn't have felt more of lonely desolation somehow, had I been robbed of a belief or had missed my destiny in life . . . Why do you sigh in this beastly way, somebody? Absurd? Well, absurd. Good Lord! mustn't a man ever – Here, give me some tobacco.' . . .

There was a pause of profound stillness, then a match flared, and Marlow's lean face appeared, worn, hollow, with downward folds and dropped eyelids, with an aspect of concentrated attention; and as he took vigorous draws at his pipe, it seemed to retreat and advance out of the night in the regular flicker of the tiny flame. The match went out.

'Absurd!' he cried. 'This is the worst of trying to tell . . . Here you all are, each moored with two good addresses, like a hulk with two anchors, a butcher round one corner, a policeman round another, excellent appetites, and temperature normal – you hear – normal from year's end to year's end. And you say, Absurd! Absurd be – exploded! Absurd! My dear boys, what can you expect from a man who out of sheer nervousness had just flung overboard a pair of new shoes. Now I think of it, it is amazing I did not shed tears. I am, upon the whole, proud of my fortitude. I was cut up to the quick* at the idea of having lost the inestimable privilege of listening to the gifted Kurtz. Of course I was wrong. The privilege was waiting for me. Oh yes, I heard more than enough. And I was right, too. A voice. He was very little more than a voice. And I heard – him – it – this voice – other voices – all of them were so little more than voices – and the memory of that time itself lingers around me, impalpable, like a dying vibration of one immense jabber, silly, atrocious, sordid, savage, or simply mean, without any kind of sense. Voices, voices – even the girl herself – now —'

He was silent for a long time.

'I laid the ghost of his gifts at last with a lie,' he began suddenly. 'Girl! What? Did I mention a girl? Oh, she is out of it – completely. They – the women I mean – are out of it – should be out of it. We must help them to stay in that beautiful world of their own, lest ours gets worse. Oh, she had to be out of it. You should have heard the disinterred body of Mr Kurtz saying, "My Intended". You would have perceived directly then how completely she was out of it. And the lofty frontal bone of Mr Kurtz! They say the hair goes on growing sometimes,* but this – ah – specimen, was impressively bald. The wilderness had patted him on the head, and, behold, it was like a ball – an ivory ball; it had caressed him, and – lo! – he had withered; it had taken him, loved him, embraced him, got into his veins, consumed his flesh, and sealed his soul to its own by the inconceivable ceremonies of some devilish initiation. He was its spoiled and pampered favourite. Ivory? I should think so. Heaps of it, stacks of it. The old mud shanty was bursting with it. You would think there was not a single tusk left either above or below the ground in the whole country. "Mostly fossil," the manager had remarked disparagingly. It was no more fossil than I am; but they call it fossil when it is dug up. It appears these niggers do bury the tusks sometimes – but evidently they couldn't bury this parcel deep enough to save the gifted Mr Kurtz from his fate. We filled the steamboat with it, and had to pile a lot on the deck. Thus he could see and enjoy as long as he could see, because the appreciation of this favour had remained with him to the last. You should have heard him say, "My ivory". Oh yes, I heard him. "My Intended, my ivory, my station, my river, my —" everything belonged to him. It made me hold my breath in expectation of hearing the wilderness burst into a prodigious peal of laughter that would shake the fixed stars in their places. Everything belonged to him – but that was a trifle. The thing was to know what he belonged to, how many powers of darkness claimed him for their own. That

was the reflection that made you creepy all over. It was impossible
– it was not good for one either – to try and imagine. He had taken
a high seat amongst the devils of the land – I mean literally. You
can't understand. How could you – with solid pavement under
your feet, surrounded by kind neighbours ready to cheer you or to
fall on you, stepping delicately between the butcher and the
policeman, in the holy terror of scandal and gallows and lunatic
asylums – how can you imagine what particular region of the first
ages a man's untrammelled feet may take him into by the way of
solitude – utter solitude without a policeman – by the way of
silence – utter silence, where no warning voice of a kind
neighbour can be heard whispering of public opinion. These little
things make all the great difference. When they are gone you must
fall back upon your own innate strength, upon your own capacity
for faithfulness. Of course you may be too much of a fool to go
wrong – too dull even to know you are being assaulted by the
powers of darkness. I take it, no fool ever made a bargain for his
soul with the devil: the fool is too much of a fool, or the devil too
much of a devil – I don't know which. Or you may be such a
thunderingly exalted creature as to be altogether deaf and blind to
anything but heavenly sights and sounds. Then the earth for you is
only a standing place – and whether to be like this is your loss or
your gain I won't pretend to say. But most of us are neither one
nor the other. The earth for us is a place to live in, where we must
put up with sights, with sounds, with smells too, by Jove! –
breathe dead hippo, so to speak, and not be contaminated. And
there, don't you see, your strength comes in, the faith in your
ability for the digging of unostentatious holes to bury the stuff in –
your power of devotion, not to yourself, but to an obscure, back-
breaking business. And that's difficult enough. Mind, I am not
trying to excuse or even explain – I am trying to account to myself
for – for – Mr Kurtz – for the shade of Mr Kurtz. This initiated
wraith from the back of Nowhere honoured me with its amazing
confidence before it vanished altogether. This was because it
could speak English to me. The original Kurtz had been educated
partly in England, and – as he was good enough to say himself –
his sympathies were in the right place. His mother was half-

English, his father was half-French.* All Europe contributed to the making of Kurtz; and by-and-by I learned that, most appropriately, the International Society for the Suppression of Savage Customs* had intrusted him with the making of a report, for their future guidance. And he had written it too. I've seen it. I've read it. It was eloquent, vibrating with eloquence, but too high-strung, I think. Seventeen pages of close writing he had found time for! But this must have been before his — let us say — nerves, went wrong, and caused him to preside at certain midnight dances ending with unspeakable rites, which — as far as I reluctantly gathered from what I heard at various times — were offered up to him — do you understand? — to Mr Kurtz himself.* But it was a beautiful piece of writing. The opening paragraph, however, in the light of later information, strikes me now as ominous. He began with the argument that we whites, from the point of development we had arrived at, "must necessarily appear to them [savages] in the nature of supernatural beings — we approach them with the might as of deity", and so on, and so on. "By the simple exercise of our will we can exert a power for good practically unbounded", etc., etc. From that point he soared and took me with him. The peroration was magnificent, though difficult to remember, you know. It gave me the notion of an exotic Immensity ruled by an august Benevolence. It made me tingle with enthusiasm. This was the unbounded power of eloquence — of words — of burning noble words. There were no practical hints to interrupt the magic current of phrases, unless a kind of note at the foot of the last page, scrawled evidently much later, in an unsteady hand, may be regarded as the exposition of a method. It was very simple, and at the end of that moving appeal to every altruistic sentiment it blazed at you, luminous and terrifying, like a flash of lightning in a serene sky: "Exterminate all the brutes!" The curious part was that he had apparently forgotten all about that valuable postscriptum, because, later on, when he in a sense came to himself, he repeatedly entreated me to take good care of "my pamphlet" (he called it), as it was sure to have in the future a good influence upon his career. I had full information about all these things and, besides, as it turned out, I was to have the care of his memory. I've done enough for it to give me the indisputable right to lay it, if I choose, for an everlasting rest in the dust-bin of progress, amongst all the sweepings and, figuratively speaking, all the dead cats of civilisation. But then, you see, I can't choose. He won't be forgotten. Whatever he was, he was not common. He had the power to charm or frighten rudimentary souls into an aggravated witch-dance in his honour; he could also fill the small souls of the pilgrims with bitter misgivings: he had one devoted friend at least, and he had conquered one soul in the world that was neither rudimentary nor tainted with self-seeking. No; I can't forget him, though I am not prepared to affirm the fellow was exactly worth the life we lost in getting to him. I missed my late helmsman awfully, – I missed him even while his body was still lying in the pilot-house. Perhaps you will think it passing strange this regret for a savage who was no more account than a grain of sand in a black Sahara. Well, don't you see, he had done something, he had steered; for months I had him at my back – a help – an instrument. It was a kind of partnership. He steered for me – I had to look after him, I worried about his deficiencies, and thus a subtle bond had been created, of which I only became aware when it was suddenly broken. And the intimate profundity of that look he gave me when he received his hurt remains to this day in my memory – like a claim of distant kinship affirmed in a supreme moment.

'Poor fool! If he had only left that shutter alone. He had no restraint, no restraint – just like Kurtz – a tree swayed by the wind. As soon as I had put on a dry pair of slippers, I dragged him out, after first jerking the spear out of his side, which operation I confess I performed with my eyes shut tight. His heels leaped together over the little doorstep; his shoulders were pressed to my breast; I hugged him from behind desperately. Oh! he was heavy, heavy; heavier than any man on earth, I should imagine. Then without more ado I tipped him overboard. The current snatched him as though he had been a wisp of grass, and I saw the body roll over twice before I lost sight of it for ever. All the pilgrims and the manager were then congregated on the awning-deck about the pilot-house, chattering at each other like a flock of excited magpies, and there was a scandalised murmur at my heartless promptitude. What they wanted to keep that body hanging about for I can't guess. Embalm it, maybe. But I had also heard another, and a very ominous, murmur on the deck below. My friends the wood-cutters were likewise scandalised, and with a better show of reason – though I admit that the reason itself was quite inadmissible. Oh, quite! I had made up my mind that if my late helmsman was to be eaten, the fishes alone should have him. He had been a very second-rate helmsman while alive, but now he was dead he might have become a first-class temptation, and possibly cause some startling trouble. Besides, I was anxious to take the wheel, the man in pink pyjamas showing himself a hopeless duffer at the business.

'This I did directly the simple funeral was over. We were going half-speed, keeping right in the middle of the stream, and I listened to the talk about me. They had given up Kurtz, they had given up the station; Kurtz was dead, and the station had been burnt – and so on – and so on. The red-haired pilgrim was beside himself with the thought that at least this poor Kurtz had been properly revenged. "Say! We must have made a glorious slaughter of them in the bush. Eh? What do you think? Say?" He positively danced, the bloodthirsty little gingery beggar. And he had nearly fainted when he saw the wounded man! I could not help saying, "You made a glorious lot of smoke, anyhow." I had seen, from the way the tops of the bushes rustled and flew, that almost all the shots had gone too high. You can't hit anything unless you take aim and fire from the shoulder; but these chaps fired from the hip with their eyes shut. The retreat, I maintained – and I was right – was caused by the screeching of the steam-whistle. Upon this they forgot Kurtz, and began to howl at me with indignant protests.

'The manager stood by the wheel murmuring confidentially about the necessity of getting well away down the river before dark at all events, when I saw in the distance a clearing on the river-side and the outlines of some sort of building. "What's this?" I asked. He clapped his hands in wonder. "The station!" he cried. I edged in at once, still going half-speed.

'Through my glasses I saw the slope of a hill interspersed with rare trees and perfectly free from undergrowth. A long decaying building on the summit was half buried in the high grass; the large holes in the peaked roof gaped black from afar; the jungle and the woods made a background. There was no enclosure or fence of any kind; but there had been one apparently, for near the house half-a-dozen slim posts remained in a row, roughly trimmed, and with their upper ends ornamented with round carved balls. The rails, or whatever there had been between, had disappeared. Of course the forest surrounded all that. The river-bank was clear, and on the water-side I saw a white man under a hat like a cart-wheel beckoning persistently with his whole arm. Examining the edge of the forest above and below, I was almost certain I could see movements – human forms gliding here and there. I steamed past prudently, then stopped the engines and let her drift down. The man on the shore began to shout, urging us to land. "We have been attacked," screamed the manager. "I know – I know. It's all right," yelled back the other, as cheerful as you please. "Come along. It's all right. I am glad."

'His aspect reminded me of something I had seen – something funny I had seen somewhere. As I manœuvred to get alongside, I was asking myself, "What does this fellow look like?" Suddenly I got it. He looked like a harlequin. His clothes had been made of some stuff that was brown holland probably, but it was covered with patches all over, with bright patches, blue, red, and yellow, – patches on the back, patches on front, patches on elbows, on knees; coloured binding round his jacket, scarlet edging at the bottom of his trousers; and the sunshine made him look extremely gay and wonderfully neat withal, because you could see how beautifully all this patching had been done. A beardless, boyish face, very fair, no features to speak of, nose peeling, little blue eyes, smiles and frowns chasing each other over that open countenance like sunshine and shadow on a wind-swept plain. "Look out, captain!" he cried; "there's a snag lodged in here last night." What! Another snag? I confess I swore shamefully. I had nearly holed my cripple, to finish off that charming trip. The harlequin on the bank turned his little pug nose up to me. "You English?" he asked, all smiles. "Are you?" I shouted from the wheel. The smiles vanished, and he shook his head as if sorry for my disappointment. Then he brightened up. "Never mind!" he cried encouragingly. "Are we in time?" I asked. "He is up there," he replied, with a toss of the head up the hill, and becoming gloomy all of a sudden. His face was like the autumn sky, overcast one moment and bright the next.

'When the manager, escorted by the pilgrims, all of them armed to the teeth, had gone to the house, this chap came on board. "I say, I don't like this. These natives are in the bush," I said. He assured me earnestly it was all right. "They are simple people," he added; "well, I am glad you came. It took me all my time to keep them off." "But you said it was all right," I cried. "Oh, they meant no harm," he said; and as I stared he corrected himself, "Not exactly." Then vivaciously, "My faith, your pilot-house wants a clean up!" In the next breath he advised me to keep enough steam on the boiler to blow the whistle in case of any trouble. "One good screech will do more for you than all your rifles. They are simple people," he repeated. He rattled away at such a rate he quite overwhelmed me. He seemed to be trying to make up for lots of silence, and actually hinted, laughing, that such was the case. "Don't you talk with Mr Kurtz?" I said. "You don't talk with that man – you listen to him," he exclaimed with severe exaltation. But now —" He waved his arm, and in the twinkling of an eye was in the uttermost depths of despondency. In a moment he came up again with a jump, possessed himself of both my hands, shook them continuously, while he gabbled: "Brother sailor . . . honour . . . pleasure . . . delight . . . introduce myself . . . Russian . . . son of an arch-priest . . . Government of Tambov . . . What? Tobacco! English tobacco; the excellent English tobacco! Now, that's brotherly. Smoke? Where's a sailor that does not smoke?"

'The pipe soothed him, and gradually I made out he had run away from school, had gone to sea in a Russian ship; ran away again; served some time in English ships; was now reconciled with the arch-priest. He made a point of that. "But when one is young one must see things, gather experience, ideas; enlarge the mind." "Here!" I interrupted. "You can never tell! Here I have met Mr Kurtz," he said, youthfully solemn and reproachful. I held my tongue after that. It appears he had persuaded a Dutch trading-house on the coast to fit him out with stores and goods, and had started for the interior with a light heart, and no more idea of what would happen to him than a baby. He had been wandering about that river for nearly two years alone, cut off from everybody and everything. "I am not so young as I look. I am twenty-five," he said. "At first old Van Shuyten* would tell me to go to the devil," he narrated with keen enjoyment; "but I stuck to him, and talked and talked, till at last he got afraid I would talk the hind-leg off his favourite dog, so he gave me some cheap things and a few guns, and told me he hoped he would never see my face again. Good old Dutchman, Van Shuyten. I've sent him one small lot of ivory a year ago, so that he can't call me a little thief when I get back. I hope he got it. And for the rest I don't care. I had some wood stacked for you. That was my old house. Did you see?"

'I gave him Towson's book. He made as though he would kiss me, but restrained himself. "The only book I had left, and I thought I had lost it," he said, looking at it ecstatically. "So many accidents happen to a man going about alone, you know. Canoes get upset sometimes – and sometimes you've got to clear out so quick when the people get angry." He thumbed the pages. "You made notes in Russian?" I asked. He nodded. "I thought they were written in cipher," I said. He laughed, then became serious. "I had lots of trouble to keep these people off," he said. "Did they want to kill you?" I asked. "Oh no!" he cried, and checked himself. "Why did they attack us?" I pursued. He hesitated, then said shamefacedly, "They don't want him to go." "Don't they?" I said, curiously. He nodded a nod full of mystery and wisdom. "I tell you," he cried, "this man has enlarged my mind." He opened his arms wide, staring at me with his little blue eyes that were perfectly round.

'I looked at him, lost in astonishment. There he was before me, in motley, as though he had absconded from a troupe of mimes; enthusiastic, fabulous. His very existence was improbable, inexplicable, and altogether bewildering. He was an insoluble problem. It was inconceivable how he had existed, how he had succeeded in getting so far, how he had managed to remain – why he did not instantly disappear. "I went a little farther," he said, "then still a little farther – till I had gone so far that I don't know how I'll ever get back. Never mind. Plenty time. I can manage. You take Kurtz away quick – quick – I tell you." The glamour of youth enveloped his particoloured rags, his destitution, his loneliness, the essential desolation of his futile wanderings. For months – for years – his life hadn't been worth a day's purchase; and there he was gallantly, thoughtlessly alive, to all appearance indestructible solely by the virtue of his few years and of his unreflecting audacity. I was seduced into something like admiration – like envy. Glamour urged him on, glamour kept him unscathed. He surely wanted nothing from the wilderness but space to breathe in and to push on through. His need was to exist, and to move onwards at the greatest possible risk, and with a maximum of privation. If the absolutely pure, uncalculating, unpractical spirit of adventure had ever ruled a human being, it ruled this be-patched youth. I almost envied him the possession of this modest and clear flame. It seemed to have consumed all thought of self so completely, that, even while he was talking to you, you forgot that it was he – the man before your eyes – who had gone through these things. I did not envy him his devotion to Kurtz, though. He had not meditated over it. It came to him, and he accepted it with a sort of eager fatalism. I must say that to me it appeared about the most dangerous thing in every way he had come upon so far.

'They had come together unavoidably, like two ships becalmed near each other, and lay rubbing sides at last. I suppose Kurtz wanted an audience, because on a certain occasion, when encamped in the forest, they had talked all night, or more probably Kurtz had talked. "We talked of everything," he said, quite transported at the recollection. "I forgot there was such a thing as sleep. The night did not seem to last an hour. Everything! Everything! . . . Of love too." "Ah, he talked to you of love!" I said, much amused. "It isn't what you think," he cried, almost passionately. "It was in general. He made me see things – things."

'He threw his arms up. We were on deck at the time, and the head-man of my wood-cutters, lounging near by, turned upon him his heavy and glittering eyes. I looked around, and I don't know why, but I assure you that never, never before, did this land, this river, this jungle, the very arch of this blazing sky, appear to me so hopeless and so dark, so impenetrable to human thought, so pitiless to human weakness. "And, ever since, you have been with him, of course?" I said.

'On the contrary. It appears their intercourse was very much broken by various causes. He had, as he informed me proudly, managed to nurse Kurtz through two illnesses (he spoke of it as you would of some risky achievement), but as a rule Kurtz wandered alone, far in the depths of the forest. "Very often coming to this station, I had to wait days and days for him to turn up," he said. "Ah, it was worth waiting for! – sometimes." "What was he doing? exploring or what?" I asked. "Oh yes, of course he had discovered lots of villages, a lake too – he did not know exactly in what direction; it was dangerous to inquire too much – but mostly his expeditions had been for ivory." "But he had no goods to trade with by that time," I objected. "There's a good lot of cartridges left even yet," he answered, looking away. "To speak plainly, he raided the country," I said. He nodded. "Not alone, surely!" He muttered something about the villages round that lake. "Kurtz got the tribe to follow him, did he?" I suggested. He fidgeted a little. "They adored him," he said. The tone of these words was so extraordinary that I looked at him searchingly. It was curious to see his mingled eagerness and reluctance to speak of Kurtz. The man filled his life, occupied his thoughts, swayed his emotions. "What can you expect!" he burst out; "he came to them with thunder and lightning, you know – and they had never seen anything like it – and very terrible. He could be very terrible. You can't judge Mr Kurtz as you would an ordinary man. No, no, no! Now – just to give you an idea – I don't mind telling you, he wanted to shoot me too one day – but I don't judge him." "Shoot you!" I cried. "What for?" "Well, I had a small lot of ivory the chief of that village near my house gave me. You see I used to shoot game for them. Well, he wanted it, and wouldn't hear reason. He said he would shoot me unless I gave him the ivory and cleared out of the country, because he could do so, and had a fancy for it, and there was nothing on earth to prevent him killing whom he jolly well pleased. And it was true too. I gave him the ivory. What did I care! But I didn't clear out. No, no. I couldn't leave him. I had to be careful, though, for a time. Then we got friendly, as before. He had his second illness then. Afterwards I had to keep out of the way again. But he was mostly living in those villages on the lake. When he came down to the river, sometimes he would take to me, and sometimes I had to keep out of his way. Just as it happened. This man suffered too much. He hated all this, and somehow he couldn't get away. When I had a chance I begged him to try and leave while there was time. I offered to go back with him. And he would say yes, and then he would remain; go off on another ivory hunt; disappear for weeks; forget himself amongst these people – forget himself – you know." "Why! he's mad," I said. He protested indignantly. Mr Kurtz couldn't be mad. If I had heard him talk, only two days ago, I wouldn't dare hint at such a thing. I had taken up my binoculars while we talked, and was looking at the shore, sweeping the limit of the forest at each side and at the back of the house. The consciousness of there being people in that bush, so silent, so quiet – as silent and quiet as the ruined house on the hill – made me uneasy. There was no sign on the face of nature of this amazing tale of cruelty and greed that was not so much told as suggested to me in desolate exclamations, completed by shrugs, in interrupted phrases, in hints ending in deep sighs. The woods were unmoved, like a mask – heavy, like the closed door of a prison – they looked with their air of hidden knowledge, of patient expectation, of unapproachable silence. The house came into the range of the glass. The Russian was telling me that it was only lately that Mr Kurtz had come down to the river, bringing along with him that lake tribe. He had been away for several months –getting himself adored, I suppose – and came down purposing a raid either across the river or down stream. Evidently the appetite for more ivory had got the better of the – what shall I say? – less material aspirations. However he had got much worse suddenly. "I heard he was lying helpless, and so I came up – took my chance," said the Russian. "Oh he is bad, very bad." I kept my glass steadily on the house. There were no signs of life, but there was the ruined roof, the long mud wall peeping above the grass, with three little square window-holes, no two of the same size; all this brought within reach of my hand, as it were. And then I made a brusque movement, and one of the remaining posts of that vanished fence leaped up in the field of my glass. You remember I told you I had been struck at the distance by certain attempts at ornamentation, rather remarkable in the ruinous neglect of the place. Now I had suddenly a nearer view, and its first result was to make me throw my head back as if before a blow. Then I went carefully from post to post with my glass, and I saw my mistake. These round knobs were not ornamental but symbolic; they were symbolic of some cruel and forbidden knowledge. They were expressive and puzzling, striking and disturbing, food for thought and also for the vultures if there had been any looking down from the sky; but at all events for such ants as were industrious enough to ascend the pole. They would have been even more impressive, those heads on the stakes,* if their faces had not been turned to the house. Only one, the first I had made out, was facing my way. I was not so shocked as you may think. The start back I had given was really nothing but a movement of surprise. I had expected to see a knob of wood there, you know. I returned deliberately to the first I had seen – and there it was, black, dried, sunken, with closed eyelids, – a head that seemed to sleep at the top of that pole, and, with the shrunken dry lips showing a narrow white line of the teeth, was smiling too, smiling continuously at some endless and jocose dream of that eternal slumber.

'I am not disclosing any trade secrets. In fact the manager said afterwards that Mr Kurtz had ruined that district. I have no opinion as to that, but I want you clearly to understand that there was nothing profitable in these heads being there. They only showed that Mr Kurtz lacked restraint in the gratification of his various lusts, that there was something wanting in him – some small matter which, when the pressing need arose, could not be found under his magnificent eloquence. Whether he knew of this deficiency himself I can't say. I think the knowledge came to him at last – only at the very last. But the wilderness had found him out early, and had taken on him a terrible vengeance for the fantastic invasion. It had tempted him with all the sinister suggestions of its loneliness. I think it had whispered to him things about himself which he did not know, things of which he had no conception till he took counsel with this great solitude – and the whisper had proved irresistibly fascinating. It echoed loudly within him because he was hollow at the core.* I put down the glass, and the head that had appeared near enough to be spoken to seemed at once to have leaped away from me into the illusion of an inaccessible distance.

'The admirer of Mr Kurtz hung his head. With a hurried, indistinct voice he began to tell me he had not dared to take these – say, symbols – down. He was not afraid of the natives; they would not move till Mr Kurtz gave the word. His ascendancy was extraordinary. The camps of these people surrounded the place, and the chiefs came every day to see him. They crawled. "I don't want to know anything of the ceremonies used when approaching Mr Kurtz," I shouted. Curious, this feeling that came over me that those details would be more intolerable to hear than those heads drying on stakes under Mr Kurtz's windows were to see. After all, that was only a savage sight, while I seemed at one bound to have been transported into some lightless region of subtle horrors, where pure, uncomplicated savagery was a positive relief, being something that had a right to exist, obviously in the sunshine. The young man looked at me with surprise. I suppose it did not occur to him Mr Kurtz was no idol of mine. He forgot I hadn't heard any of these splendid monologues on, what was it? on love, justice, conduct of life – or what not. If it had come to crawling before Mr Kurtz, he crawled as much as the veriest savage of them all. I had no idea of the conditions, he said: these heads were the heads of rebels. I shocked him excessively by laughing. Rebels! What would be the next definition I was to hear? There had been enemies, criminals, workers – and these were rebels. Those rebellious heads looked very pacific to me on their sticks. "You don't know how such a life tries a man like Kurtz," cried Kurtz's last disciple. "Well, and you?" I said. "I! I! I am a simple man. I have no great thoughts. I want nothing from anybody. How can you compare me to . . .?" His feelings were too much for speech, and suddenly he broke down. "I don't understand," he groaned. "I've been doing my best to keep him alive, and that's enough. I had no hand in all this. I have no abilities. There hasn't been a drop of medicine or a mouthful of invalid food for months here. He was shamefully abandoned. A man like this, with such ideas. Shamefully! Shamefully! I – I – haven't slept for the last ten nights . . ."

'His voice lost itself in the calm of the evening. The long shadows of the forest had slipped down hill while we talked, had gone far beyond the ruined hovel, beyond the symbolic row of stakes. All this was in the gloom, while we down there were yet in the sunshine, and the stretch of the river abreast of the clearing glittered in a still and dazzling splendour, with a murky and overshadowed band above and below. Not a living soul was seen on the shore. The bushes did not rustle.

'Suddenly round the corner of the house a group of men appeared. It was as though they had come up from the ground. They waded waist-deep in the grass, in a compact body, bearing an improvised stretcher in their midst. Instantly, in the emptiness of the landscape, a cry arose whose shrillness pierced the still air like a sharp arrow flying straight to the very heart of the land; and, as if by enchantment, streams of human beings – of naked human beings – with spears in their hands, with bows, with shields, with wild glances and savage movements, were poured into the clearing by the dark-faced and pensive forest. The bushes shook, the grass swayed for a time, and then everything stood still in attentive immobility.

' "Now, if he does not speak to them we are all done for," said the Russian at my elbow. The knot of men with the stretcher had stopped too, halfway to the steamer, as if petrified. I saw the man on the stretcher sit up, lank and with an uplifted arm, above the shoulders of the bearers. "Let us hope that the man who can talk so well of love in general will find some particular reason to spare us this time," I said. I resented bitterly the absurd danger of our situation, as if to be at the mercy of the atrocious phantom who ruled this land had been a dishonouring necessity. I could not hear anything, but through my glasses I saw the thin arm extended commandingly, the lower jaw moving, the eyes of that apparition shining darkly far in his bony head that nodded with grotesque jerks. Kurtz – Kurtz – that means short in German – don't it? Well, the name was as true as everything else in his life – and death. He looked at least seven feet long. His covering had fallen off, and his body emerged from it pitiful and appalling as from a winding-sheet. I could see the cage of his ribs all astir, the bones of his arm waving. It was as though an animated image of death carved out of old ivory had been shaking its hand with menaces at a motionless crowd of men made of dark and glittering bronze. I saw him open his mouth wide – it gave him a weirdly voracious aspect, as though he had wanted to swallow all the air, all the earth, all the men before him. A deep sound reached me faintly. He must have been shouting. He fell back suddenly. The stretcher shook as the bearers staggered forward again, and almost at the same time I noticed that the crowd of savages had already diminished, was vanishing without any perceptible movement of retreat, as if the forest that had ejected these beings so suddenly had drawn them in again as the breath is drawn in a long aspiration.

'Some of the pilgrims behind the stretcher carried his arms – two shot-guns, a heavy rifle, and a light revolver-carbine – the thunderbolts of that pitiful Jupiter. The manager bent over him murmuring as he walked beside his head. They laid him down in one of the little cabins, just a room for a bed-place and a camp-stool or two, you know. We had brought his belated correspondence, and a lot of torn envelopes and open letters littered his bed. His hand roamed feebly amongst these papers. I was struck by the fire of his eyes and the composed languor of his expression. It was not so much the exhaustion of disease. He did not seem in pain. This shadow looked satiated and calm, as though for the moment it had had its fill of all the emotions.

'He rustled one of the letters, and looking in my face said, "I am glad." Somebody had been writing to him about me. These special recommendations again. The volume of tone he emitted without effort, almost without the trouble of moving his lips, amazed me. A voice! a voice! It was grave, profound, vibrating, while the man did not seem capable of a whisper. However, he had enough strength in him – factitious no doubt – to very nearly make an end of us, as you shall hear directly.

'The manager appeared in the doorway, so I stepped out at once and he drew the curtain after me. The Russian, eyed curiously by the pilgrims, was staring at the shore. I followed the direction of his glance.

'Several bronze figures could be made out in the distance, moving indistinctly against the gloomy border of the forest, and near the river two were standing leaning on spears in the sunlight, under fantastic head-dresses of spotted skins, warlike, and still in statuesque repose. And from right to left along the lighted shore moved a wild and gorgeous apparition of a woman.

'She walked with measured steps, draped in striped and fringed cloths, treading the earth proudly, with a slight jingle and flash of barbarous ornaments. She carried her head high; her hair was done in the shape of a helmet; she had brass leggings to the knee, brass wire gauntlets to the elbow, a crimson spot on her tawny cheek, innumerable necklaces of glass beads on her neck; bizarre things, charms, gifts of witch-men, that hung about her, glittered and trembled at every step. She must have had the value of several elephant tusks upon her. She was savage and superb, wild-eyed and magnificent; there was something ominous and stately in her deliberate progress. And in the hush that had fallen suddenly upon the whole sorrowful land, the immense wilderness, the colossal body of the fecund and mysterious life seemed to look at her as though it had been looking at the image of its own tenebrous and passionate soul.

'And we men also looked at her – at any rate I looked at her. She came abreast of the steamer, stood still, and faced us. Her long shadow fell to the water's edge. Her face had a tragic and fierce aspect of wild sorrow and of dumb fear mingled with the pain of a struggling, half-shaped emotion. She stood looking at us without a stir, and like the wilderness itself with an air of brooding over an inscrutable purpose. A whole minute passed, and then she made a step forward. There was a low jingle, a glint of yellow metal, a sway of fringed draperies, and she stopped. Had her heart failed her, or had her eyes, veiled with that mournfulness that lies over all the wild things of the earth, seen the hopelessness of longing that will find out sometimes even a savage soul in the lonely darkness of its being? Who can tell. Perhaps she did not know herself. The young fellow by my side growled. The pilgrims murmured at my back. She looked at us all as if her life depended upon the unswerving steadiness of her glance. Suddenly she opened her bared arms and threw them up rigid above her head, as though in an uncontrollable desire to touch the sky, and at the same time the shadows of her arms darted out on the earth, swept around on the river, gathering the steamer into a shadowy embrace. Her sudden gesture seemed to demand a cry, but the unbroken silence that hung over the scene was more formidable than any sound could be.

'She turned, walked on, following the bank, and passed into the bushes to the left. Once only her eyes gleamed back at us in the dusk of the thickets and she disappeared.

' "If she had offered to come aboard I think I would have tried to shoot her," said the man of patches, nervously. "I had been risking my life every day for the last fortnight to keep her out of the house. She got in once and kicked up a row about those miserable rags I picked up in the storeroom to mend my clothes with. I was not decent. At least it must have been that, for she talked to Kurtz for an hour, pointing at me now and then. I don't understand the dialect of this tribe. Luckily for me, Kurtz felt too ill that day to care, or there would have been mischief. I don't understand . . . No – it's too much for me. Ah, well, it's all over now."

'At this moment I heard Kurtz's deep voice behind the curtain, "Save me! – save the ivory, you mean. Don't tell me. Save me! Why, I've had to save you. You are interrupting my plans now. Sick! Sick! Not so sick as you would like to believe. Never mind. I'll carry my ideas out yet – I will return. I'll show you what can be done. You with your little peddling notions – you are interfering with me. I will return. I . . ."

'The manager came out. He did me the honour to take me under the arm and lead me aside. "He is very low, very low," he said. He considered it necessary to sigh, but forgot to be consistently sorrowful. "We have done all we could for him – haven't we? But there is no disguising the fact, Mr Kurtz has done more harm than good to the Company. He did not see the time was not ripe for vigorous action. Cautiously, cautiously, that's my principle. We must be cautious yet. The district is closed to us for a time. Deplorable! Upon the whole, the trade will suffer. I don't deny there is a remarkable quantity of ivory – mostly fossil. We must save it, at all events – but look how precarious the position is – and why? Because the method is unsound." "Do you," said I, looking at the shore, "call it 'unsound method'?" "Without doubt," he exclaimed, hotly. "Don't you?" "No method at all," I murmured. "Exactly," he exulted. "I anticipated this. A complete want of judgment. It is my duty to point it out in the proper quarter." "Oh," said I, "that fellow – what's his name? – the brickmaker, will make a readable report for you." He appeared confounded for a moment. It seemed to me I had never breathed an atmosphere so vile, and I turned mentally to Kurtz for relief – positively for relief. "Nevertheless I think Mr Kurtz is a remarkable man," I said with emphasis. He started, dropped on me a cold heavy glance, said very quietly, "He *was*," and turned his back on me. My hour of favour was over. I found myself lumped along with Kurtz as a partisan of methods for which the time was not ripe. I was unsound. Ah! but it was something to have at least a choice of nightmares.

'I had turned to the wilderness really, not to Mr Kurtz, who, I was ready to admit, was as good as buried. And for a moment it seemed to me as if I also were buried in a vast grave full of unspeakable secrets. I felt an intolerable weight oppressing my breast, the smell of the damp earth, the unseen presence of victorious corruption, the darkness of an impenetrable night. The Russian tapped me on the shoulder. I heard him mumbling and stammering something about "brother seaman – couldn't conceal – knowledge of matters that would affect Mr Kurtz's reputation". I waited. For him evidently Mr Kurtz was not in his grave. I suspect that for him Mr Kurtz was one of the immortals. "Well!" said I at last, "speak out. As it happens, I am Mr Kurtz's friend – in a way."

'He stated with a good deal of formality that had we not been "of the same profession", he would have kept the matter to himself without regard to consequences. He suspected there was an active ill-will towards him on the part of these white men that —" "You are right," I said, remembering a certain conversation I had overheard. "The manager thinks you ought to be hanged." He showed a concern at this intelligence which astonished me at first. "I had better get out of the way quietly," he said, earnestly. "I can do no more for Kurtz now, and they would soon find a pretext . . . What's to stop them? There's a military post three hundred miles from here." "Well, upon my word," said I, "Perhaps you had better go if you have any friends amongst the savages near by." "Plenty," he said. "They are simple people –and I want nothing, you know." He stood biting his lip, then: "I don't want any harm to happen to these whites here, but of course I was thinking of Mr Kurtz's reputation – but you are a brother seaman and—" "All right," said I, after a time. "Mr Kurtz's reputation is safe with me." I did not know how truly I spoke.

'He informed me, lowering his voice, that it was Kurtz who had ordered the attack to be made on the steamer. "He hated sometimes the idea of being taken away – and then again . . . But I don't understand these matters. I am a simple man. He thought it would scare you away – that you would give it up, thinking him dead. I could not stop him. Oh, I had an awful time of it this last month." "Very well," I said. "He is all right now," "Ye-e-es," he muttered, not very convinced apparently. "Thanks," said I; "I shall keep my eyes open." "But quiet – eh?" he urged, anxiously. "It would be awful for his reputation if anybody here . . ." I promised a complete discretion with great gravity. "I have a canoe and three black fellows not very far. I am off. Could you give me a few Martini-Henry cartridges?" I could, and did, with proper secrecy. He helped himself, with a wink at me, to a handful of my tobacco. "Between sailors – you know – good English tobacco." At the door of the pilot-house he turned round – "I say, haven't you a pair of shoes you could spare?" He raised one leg. "Look." The soles were tied with knotted strings sandal-wise under his bare feet. I rooted out an old pair, at which he looked with admiration before tucking them under his left arm. One of his pockets (bright red) was bulging with cartridges, from the other (dark blue) peeped "Towson's Inquiry", etc., etc. He seemed to think himself excellently well equipped for a renewed encounter with the wilderness. "Ah! I'll never, never meet such a man again. You ought to have heard him recite poetry – his own too it was, he told me. Poetry!" He rolled his eyes at the recollection of these delights. "Oh, he enlarged my mind!" "Good-bye," said I. He shook hands and vanished in the night. I ask myself whether I had ever really seen him – whether it was possible to meet such a phenomenon.

'When I woke up shortly after midnight his warning came to my mind with its hint of danger that seemed, in the starred darkness, real enough to make me get up for the purpose of having a look round. On the hill a big fire burned, illuminating fitfully a crooked corner of the station-house. One of the agents with a picket of a few of our blacks, armed for the purpose, was keeping guard. But deep within the forest, red gleams that wavered, that seemed to sink and rise from the ground amongst confused columnar shapes of intense blackness, showed the exact position of the camp where Mr Kurtz's adorers were keeping their uneasy vigil. The monotonous beating of a big drum filled the air with muffled shocks and a lingering vibration. A steady droning sound of many men chanting each to himself some weird incantation came out from the black, flat wall of the woods as the humming of bees comes out of a hive, and had a strange narcotic effect upon my half-awake senses. I believe I dozed off leaning over the rail, till an abrupt burst of yells, an overwhelming outbreak of a pent-up and mysterious frenzy, woke me up in a bewildered wonder. It was cut short all at once, and the low droning went on with an effect of audible and soothing silence. I glanced casually into the little cabin. A light was burning. Kurtz was not there.

'I think I would have raised an outcry if I had believed my eyes. But I didn't believe them at first, the thing seemed so impossible. The fact is I was completely unnerved. Sheer blank fright, pure abstract terror, unconnected with any distinct shape of physical danger. What made this emotion so overpowering was – how shall I define it? – the moral shock I received, as if something altogether monstrous, intolerable to thought, odious to the soul, had been thrust upon me unexpectedly. This lasted of course the merest fraction of a second, and then the usual sense of commonplace, deadly danger, the possibility of a sudden on-slaught and massacre, or something of the kind, which I saw impending, was positively welcome and composing. It pacified me, in fact, and I did not raise an alarm.

'There was an agent buttoned up inside an ulster sleeping on a chair on deck within three feet of me. The yells had not awakened him, and he snored very slightly. I left him to his slumbers and leaped ashore. I did not betray Mr Kurtz – it was ordered I should never betray him – it was written I should be loyal to the nightmare of my choice. I was anxious to deal with this shadow by myself alone, – and to this day I don't know why I was so jealous of sharing with any one the dismal blackness of this experience.

'As soon as I got on the bank I saw a trail – a broad trail through the grass. I remember the exultation with which I said to myself, "He can't walk – he is crawling – I've got him." The grass was wet with dew. I strode rapidly with clenched fists. I fancy I had some vague notion of falling upon him and giving him a drubbing. I don't know. I had some imbecile thoughts. The knitting old woman with the cat obtruded herself upon me as a most improper person to be sitting at the other end of such an affair. I saw a row of pilgrims squirting lead in the air out of Winchesters held to the hip. I thought I would never get back to the steamer, and saw myself living alone and unarmed in the woods to an advanced age. Such silly things – you know. And I remember I confounded the beat of the drum with the beating of my heart, and was pleased at its calm regularity.

'I kept to the track though – then stopped to listen. The night was very clear: a dark blue space, sparkling with dew and starlight, where black things stood very still. I thought I saw a kind of motion ahead of me. I was strangely cocksure of everything that night. I actually left the track and ran in a wide semicircle, I verily believe chuckling to myself, so as to get in front of that stir, of that motion I had seen – if indeed I had seen anything. I was circumventing Kurtz as if it had been a boyish game for fun.

'I came upon him, and, if he had not heard me coming, I would have fallen over him too; but he got up in time in front of me. He rose, unsteady, long, pale, indistinct, like a vapour exhaled by the earth, and swayed slightly, misty and silent before me; while at my back the fires loomed between the trees, and the murmur of many voices issued from the forest. I had cut him off cleverly; but when actually confronting him I seemed to come to my senses, I saw the danger in its right proportion. It was by no means over yet. Suppose he began to shout. Though he could hardly stand, there was still plenty of vigour in his voice. "Go away – hide yourself," he said, in that profound tone. It was very awful. I glanced back. We were within thirty yards from the nearest fire. A black figure stood up, strode on long black legs, waving long black arms, across the glow. It had horns – antelope horns, I think – on its head. Some sorcerer, some witchman, no doubt: it looked fiend-like enough. "Do you know what you are doing?" I whispered. "Perfectly," he answered, raising his voice for that single word: it sounded to me far off and yet loud, like a hail through a speaking-trumpet. If he makes a row we are lost, I thought to myself. This clearly was not a case for fisticuffs, even apart from the very natural aversion I had to beat that Shadow – this wandering and tormented thing, that seemed released from one grave only to sink for ever into another. "You will be lost," I said – "utterly lost." One gets sometimes such a flash of inspiration, you know. I did say the right thing, though indeed he could not have been more irretrievably lost than he was at this very moment, when the foundations of our intimacy were being laid – to endure – to endure – even to the end – even beyond.

' "I had immense plans," he muttered irresolutely. "Yes," said I; "but if you try to shout I'll smash your head with —" there was not a stick or a stone near. "I will throttle you for good," I corrected myself. "I was on the threshold of great things," he pleaded, in a voice of longing, with a wistfulness of tone that made my blood run cold. "And now for this stupid scoundrel —" "Your success in Europe is assured in any case," I affirmed, steadily. I did not want to have the throttling of him, you understand – and indeed it would have been very little use for any practical purpose. I tried to break the spell – the heavy, mute spell of the wilderness – that seemed to draw him to its pitiless breast by the awakening of forgotten and brutal instincts, by the memory of gratified and monstrous passions. This alone, I was convinced, had driven him out to the edge of the forest, to the bush, towards the gleam of fires, the throb of drums, the drone of weird incantations; this alone had beguiled his unlawful soul beyond the bounds of permitted aspirations. And, don't you see, the terror of the position was not in being knocked on the head – though I had a very lively sense of that danger too – but in this, that I had to deal with a being to whom I could not appeal in the name of anything high or low. I had, even like the niggers, to invoke him – himself – his own exalted and incredible degradation. There was nothing either above or below him, and I knew it. He had kicked himself loose of the earth. Confound the man! he had kicked the very earth to pieces. He was alone, and I before him did not know whether I stood on the ground or floated in the air. I've been telling you what we said – repeating the phrases we pronounced, – but what's the good? They were common everyday words, – the familar, vague sounds exchanged on every waking day of life. But what of that? They had behind them, to my mind, the terrific suggestiveness of words heard in dreams, of phrases spoken in nightmares. Soul! If anybody had ever struggled with a soul, I am the man. And I wasn't arguing with a madman either. Believe me or not, his intelligence was perfectly clear – concentrated, it is true, upon himself with horrible intensity, yet clear; and therein was my only chance – barring, of course, the killing him there and then, which wasn't so good, on account of unavoidable noise. But his soul was mad. Being alone in the wilderness, it had looked within itself, and, by heavens! I tell you, it had gone mad. I had – for my sins, I suppose – to go through the ordeal of looking into it myself. No eloquence could have been so withering as his final burst of sincerity. He struggled with himself, too. I saw it, – I heard it. I saw the inconceivable mystery of a soul that knew no restraint, no faith, and no fear, yet struggling blindly with itself. I kept my head pretty well; but when I had him at last stretched on the couch, I wiped my forehead, while my legs shook under me as though I had carried half a ton on my back down that hill. And yet I had only supported him, his bony arm clasped round my neck, and he was not much heavier than a child.

'And when next day we left at noon, the crowd, of whose presence behind the curtain of trees I had been acutely conscious all the time, flowed out of the woods again, filled the clearing, covered the slope with a mass of naked, breathing, quivering bronze bodies. I steamed up a bit, then swung down-stream, and two thousand eyes followed the evolutions of the splashing, thumping, fierce river-demon beating the water with its terrible tail and breathing black smoke into the air. In front of the first rank, along the river, three men, plastered with bright red earth from head to foot, strutted to and fro restlessly. When we came abreast again, they faced the river, stamped their feet, nodded their horned heads, swayed their scarlet bodies; they shook towards the same river-demon a bunch of black feathers, a spotted skin with a pendent tail – something that looked like a dried gourd; they shouted periodically together strings of amazing words that resembled no sounds of human language; and the deep murmurs of the crowd, interrupted suddenly, were like the responses of some satanic litany.

'We had carried Kurtz into the pilot-house: there was more air there. Lying on the couch, he stared through the open shutter. There was an eddy in the mass of black heads, and the woman with helmeted head and tawny cheeks rushed out to the very brink of the stream. She put out her hands, shouted something, and all that wild mob took up the shout in an amazing chorus of articulated, rapid, breathless utterance.

' "Do you understand this?" I asked.

'He kept on looking out with fiery, longing eyes, with a mingled expression of wistfulness and hate. He did not answer me, but at my question I saw a smile, a smile of indefinable meaning, appear on his colourless lips that a moment after twitched convulsively with pain or rage. "I will return," he said, slowly, gasping as if the words of promise and menace had been torn out of him by a supernatural power.

'I pulled the string of the whistle, and I did this because I saw the pilgrims on deck getting out their rifles with an air of anticipating a jolly lark. At the sudden screech there was a movement of abject terror through that wedged mass of bodies. "Don't! don't! you frighten them away," cried some one on deck disconsolately. I pulled the string again and again. They broke and ran, they leaped, they crouched, they swerved, as if dodging the terrible sound. The three red chaps had fallen flat, face down on the shore, as though they had been shot dead. Only the barbarous and superb woman did not so much as flinch, and stretched tragically her bare arms after us over the brown and glittering river.

'And then that imbecile crowd down on the deck started their little fun, and I could see nothing more for smoke.

'The brown current ran swiftly out of the heart of darkness, bearing us down towards the sea with twice the speed of our upward progress; and Kurtz's life was running swiftly too, ebbing, ebbing out of his heart into the sea of inexorable time. The manager was very placid. He had no vital anxieties now. He took in both of us in a comprehensive and satisfied glance. The "affair" had come off as well as could be wished. I saw the time approaching when I would be left alone of the party of "unsound method". The pilgrims looked upon me with disfavour. I was, so to speak, numbered with the dead. It is strange how I accepted this unforeseen partnership, this choice of nightmares forced upon me in the tenebrous land invaded by these mean and greedy phantoms.

'Kurtz discoursed. A voice! a voice! It rang deep to the very last. It survived his strength to hide in the magnificent folds of eloquence the barren darkness of his heart. Oh, he struggled! he struggled! The wastes of his weary brain were haunted by shadowy images now – images of wealth and fame revolving obsequiously round his unextinguishable gift of noble and lofty expression. My Intended, my station, my career, my ideas – these were the subjects for the occasional utterances of elevated sentiments. The shade of the original Kurtz frequented the bedside of the hollow sham, whose fate it was to be buried presently in the mould of primeval earth. But both the diabolic love and the unearthly hate of the mysteries it had penetrated fought for the possession of that soul satiated with primitive emotions, avid of lying fame, of sham distinction, of all the appearances of success and power.

'Sometimes he was contemptibly childish. He desired to have kings meet him at railway stations on his return from some ghastly Nowhere, where he intended to accomplish great things. "You show them you have in you something that is really profitable, and then there will be no limits to the recognition of your ability," he would say. "Of course you must take care of the motives – right motives – always." The long reaches that were like one and the same reach, monotonous bends that were exactly alike, slipped past the steamer with their multitude of secular trees looking patiently after this grimy fragment of another world, the forerunner of change, of conquest, of trade, of massacres, of blessings. I looked ahead – piloting. "Close the shutter," said Kurtz suddenly one day; "I can't bear to look at this." I did so. There was a silence. "Oh, but I will wring your heart yet!" he cried at the invisible wilderness.

'We broke down – as I had expected – and had to lie up for

repairs at the head of an island. This delay was the first thing that shook Kurtz's confidence. One morning he gave me a packet of papers and a photograph, – the lot tied together with a shoe-string. "Keep this for me," he said. "This noxious fool" (meaning the manager) "is capable of prying into my boxes when I am not looking." In the afternoon I saw him. He was lying on his back with closed eyes, and I withdrew quietly, but I heard him mutter, "Live rightly, die, die . . ."* I listened. There was nothing more. Was he rehearsing some speech in his sleep, or was it a fragment of a phrase from some newspaper article? He had been writing for the papers and meant to do so again, "for the furthering of my ideas. It's a duty."

'His was an impenetrable darkness. I looked at him as you peer down at a man who is lying at the bottom of a precipice where the sun never shines. But I had not much time to give him, because I was helping the engine-driver to take to pieces the leaky cylinders, to straighten a bent connecting-rod, and in other such matters. I lived in a repulsive mess of nuts, bolts, spanners, hammers, ratchets – things I abominate, because I don't get on with them. I tended the little forge we fortunately had aboard; I toiled wearily in a wretched scrap heap, unless I had the shakes too bad to stand.

'One evening coming in with a candle I was startled to hear him say a little querulously, "I am lying here in the dark waiting for death." The light was within a foot of his eyes. I managed to murmur, "Oh, nonsense!" and stood over him as if transfixed.

'Anything approaching the expression that came over his face I have never seen before, and hope never to see again. Oh, I wasn't touched. I was fascinated. It was as though a veil had been rent.* I saw on that ivory face the expression of strange pride, of mental power, of avarice, of blood-thirstiness, of cunning, of excessive terror, of an intense and hopeless despair. Did he live his life through in every detail of desire, temptation, and surrender during that supreme moment of complete knowledge? He cried whisperingly at some image, at some vision, – he cried twice, with a cry that was no more than a breath—

' "The horror! The horror!"*

'I blew the candle out and left the cabin. The pilgrims were dining in the mess-cabin. I took my place opposite the manager, who lifted his eyes to give me a questioning glance, which I successfully ignored. He leaned back, serene, with that peculiar smile of his sealing the unexpressed depths of his meanness. A continuous shower of small flies streamed upon the lamp, upon the cloth, upon our hands and faces. Suddenly the manager's boy put his insolent black face in the doorway, and said in a tone of scathing contempt –

' "Mistah Kurtz – he dead."

'All the pilgrims rushed out to see. I remained, and went on with my dinner. I believe I was considered brutally callous. However, I did not eat much. There was a lamp in there – light, don't you know – and outside it was so beastly, beastly dark. I went no more near the remarkable man who had so unhesitatingly pronounced a judgment upon the adventures of his soul on this earth. The voice was gone. What else had been there? But I am of course aware that next day the pilgrims buried something in a muddy hole.

'And then they very nearly buried me.*

'However, as you see, I did not go to join Kurtz there and then. I did not. I remained to dream the nightmare out to the end, and to show my loyalty to Kurtz once more. Destiny. My destiny! Droll thing life is – that mysterious arrangement of merciless logic for a futile purpose. The most you can hope from it is some knowledge of yourself – that comes too late – a crop of unextinguishable regrets. I have wrestled with death. It is the most unexciting contest you can imagine. It takes place in an impalpable greyness, with nothing underfoot, with nothing around, without spectators, without clamour, without glory, without the great desire of victory, without the great fear of defeat, in a sickly atmosphere of tepid scepticism, without much belief in your own right, and still less in that of your adversary. If such is the form of ultimate wisdom, then life is a greater riddle than some of us think it to be. I was within a hair's-breadth of the last opportunity for pronouncement, and I found with humiliation that probably I would have nothing to say. That is the reason why I affirm that Kurtz was a remarkable man. He had something to say. He said it. Since I had peeped over the edge myself, I understand better the meaning of his stare, that could not see the flame of the candle, but was wide enough to embrace the whole universe, piercing enough to penetrate all the hearts that beat in the darkness. He had summed up – he had judged. "The horror!" He was a remarkable man. After all, this was the expression of some sort of belief. It had candour, it had conviction, it had a vibrating note of revolt in its whisper, it had the appalling face of a glimpsed truth – the strange commingling of desire and hate. And it is not my own extremity I remember best – a vision of greyness without form filled with physical pain, and a careless contempt for the evanescence of all things – even of this pain itself. No! It is his extremity that I seem to have lived through. True, he had made that last stride, he had stepped over the edge, while I had been permitted to draw back my hesitating foot. And perhaps in this is the whole difference; perhaps all the wisdom, and all truth, and all sincerity, are just compressed into that inappreciable moment of time in which we step over the threshold of the invisible. Perhaps! I like to think my summing-up would not have been a word of careless contempt. Better his cry – much better. It was an affirmation, a moral victory paid for by innumerable defeats, by abominable terrors, by abominable satisfactions. But it was a victory. That is why I have remained loyal to Kurtz to the last, and even beyond, when long time after I heard once more, not his own voice, but the echo of his magnificent eloquence thrown to me from a soul as translucently pure as a cliff of crystal.

'No, they did not bury me, though there is a period of time which I remember mistily, with a shuddering wonder, like a passage through some inconceivable world that had no hope in it and no desire. I found myself in the sepulchral city resenting the sight of people hurrying through the streets to filch a little money from each other or to devour their infamous cookery, to gulp their unwholesome beer, to dream their insignificant and silly dreams. They trespassed upon my thoughts. They were intruders whose knowledge of life was to me an irritating pretence, because I felt so sure they could not possibly know the things I knew; and their bearing, which was simply the bearing of commonplace individuals going about their business in the assurance of perfect safety, was offensive to me like the outrageous flauntings of folly in the face of a danger it is unable to comprehend. I had no particular desire to enlighten them, but I had some difficulty in restraining myself from laughing in their faces, so full of stupid importance. I daresay I was not very well at that time. I tottered about the streets — there were various affairs to settle — grinning bitterly at perfectly respectable persons. I admit my behaviour was inexcusable, but then my temperature was seldom normal in these days. My dear aunt's endeavours to "nurse up my strength" seemed altogether beside the mark. It was not my strength that wanted nursing, it was really my imagination that wanted soothing. I kept the bundle of papers given me by Kurtz, not knowing exactly what to do with it. His mother had died lately, watched over, as I was told, by his Intended. A clean-shaved man, with an official manner and wearing gold-rimmed spectacles, called on me one day and made inquiries, at first circuitous, afterwards suavely pressing, about what he was pleased to denominate certain "documents". I was not very surprised, because I had two rows with the manager on the subject out there. I had refused to give up the smallest scrap out of that package to him, and I took the same attitude with the spectacled man. He became darkly menacing at last, and with much heat argued that the Company had the right to every bit of information about their "territories". And, said he, "Mr Kurtz's knowledge of unexplored regions must have been necessarily extensive and peculiar — owing to his great abilities and to the deplorable circumstances in which he had been placed: therefore —" I assured him Mr Kurtz's knowledge, however extensive, did not bear upon the problems of commerce or administration. He invoked then the name of science. "It would be an incalculable loss if," etc., etc. I offered him the report on the "Suppression of Savage Customs", with the *post-scriptum* torn off. He took it up eagerly, but ended by sniffing at it with an air of contempt. "This is not what we had a right to expect," he remarked. "Expect nothing else," I said. "There are only private letters." He withdrew upon some threat of legal proceedings, and I saw him no more; but another fellow, calling himself Kurtz's cousin, appeared two days later, and was anxious to hear all the details about his dear relative's last moments. Incidentally he gave me to understand that Kurtz had been essentially a great musician. "There was the making of an immense success," said the man, who was an organist, I believe, with lank grey hair flowing over a greasy coat-collar. I had no reason to doubt his statement; and to this day I am unable to say what was Kurtz's profession, whether he ever had any – which was the greatest of his talents. I had thought him a painter who wrote for the papers, or a journalist who could paint – but even the cousin (who took snuff during the interview) could not tell me what he had been – exactly. He was a universal genius – on that point I agreed with the old chap, who thereupon blew his nose noisily into a large cotton handkerchief and withdrew in senile agitation, bearing off some family letters and memoranda without importance. Ultimately a journalist anxious to know something of the fate of his "dear colleague" turned up. This visitor informed me Kurtz's real sphere ought to have been politics "on the popular side". He had furry straight eyebrows, bristly hair cropped short, an eye-glass on a broad ribbon, and, becoming expansive, confessed his opinion that Kurtz couldn't write a bit – "but heavens! how that man could talk! He electrified large meetings. He had faith – don't you see? – he had the faith. He could believe anything – anything. He would have been a splendid leader of an extreme party."* "What party?" I asked. "Any party," answered the other. "He was an – an – extremist." Did I not think so? I assented. Did I know, he asked, with a sudden flash of curiosity, "what induced him to go out there?" "Yes," said I, and forthwith handed him the famous Report for publication, if he thought fit. He glanced through it hurriedly, mumbling all the time, judged "it would do", and took himself off with his plunder.

'Thus I was left at last with a slim packet of letters and the girl's portrait. She struck me as beautiful – I mean she had a beautiful expression. I know that the sunlight can be made to lie too, yet that face on paper seemed to be a reflection of truth itself. One felt that no manipulation of light and pose could have conveyed the delicate shade of truthfulness upon those features. She looked out truthfully. She seemed ready to listen without mental reservation, without suspicion, without a thought for herself. I concluded I would go and give her back her portrait and those letters myself. Curiosity? Yes; and also some other feeling perhaps.* All that had been Kurtz's had passed out of my hands: his soul, his body, his station, his plans, his ivory, his career. There remained only his memory and his Intended — and I wanted to give that up too to the past, in a way, — to surrender personally all that remained of him with me to that oblivion which is the last word of our common fate. I don't defend myself. I had no clear perception of what it was I really wanted. Perhaps it was an impulse of unconscious loyalty, or the fulfilment of one of these ironic necessities that lurk in the facts of human existence. I don't know. I can't tell. But I went.

'I thought his memory was like other memories of the dead that accumulate in every man's life, — a vague impress on the brain of shadows that had fallen on it in their swift and final passage; but before the high and ponderous door, between the tall houses of a street as still and decorous as a well-kept sepulchre, I had a vision of him on the stretcher, opening his mouth voraciously, as if to devour all the earth with all its mankind. He lived then before me; he lived as much as he had ever lived — a shadow insatiable of splendid appearances, of frightful realities; a shadow darker than the shadow of the night, and draped nobly in the folds of a gorgeous eloquence. The vision seemed to enter the house with me, the stretcher, the phantom-bearers; the wild crowd of obedient worshippers; the gloom of the forests; the glitter of the reach between the murky bends; the beat of the drum, regular and muffled like the beating of a heart — the heart of a conquering darkness. It was a moment of triumph for the wilderness, an invading and vengeful rush which, it seemed to me, I would have to keep back alone for the salvation of another soul. And the memory of what I had heard him say afar there, with the horned shapes stirring at my back, in the glow of fires, within the patient woods, those broken phrases came back to me, were heard again in their ominous and terrifying simplicity: "I have lived — supremely!" "What do you want here? I have been dead — and

damned." "Let me go – I want more of it." More of what? More
blood, more heads on stakes, more adoration, rapine, and
murder. I remembered his abject pleading, his abject threats, the
colossal scale of his vile desires, the meanness, the torment, the
tempestuous anguish of his soul. And later on his collected
languid manner, when he said one day, "This lot of ivory now is
really mine. The Company did not pay for it. I collected it myself
at my personal risk. I am afraid they will claim it as theirs. It is a
difficult case. What do you think I ought to do – resist? Eh? I want
no more than justice." He wanted no more than justice. No more
than justice. I rang the bell before a mahogany door on the first
floor, and while I waited he seemed to stare at me out of the
gleaming panel* – stare with that wide and immense stare
embracing, condemning, loathing all the universe. I seemed to
hear the whispered cry, "The horror! The horror!"

'The dusk was falling. I had to wait in a lofty drawing-room
with three long windows from floor to ceiling that were like three
luminous and bedraped columns. The bent gilt legs and backs of
the furniture shone in indistinct curves. The tall marble fireplace
had a cold and heavy whiteness. A grand piano stood massively in
a corner, with dark gleams on the flat surfaces like a sombre and
polished sarcophagus. A high door opened – closed. I rose.

'She came forward, all in black, with a pale head, floating
towards me in the dusk. She was in mourning. It was more than a
year since his death, more than a year since the news came; she
seemed as though she would remember and mourn for ever. She
took both my hands in hers and murmured, "I had heard you were
coming." I noticed she was not very young – I mean not girlish.
She had a mature capacity for fidelity, for belief, for suffering. The
room seemed to have grown darker, as if all the sad light of the
cloudy evening had taken refuge on her forehead. This fair hair,
this pale visage, this pure brow, seemed surrounded by an ashy
halo from which the dark eyes looked out at me. Their glance was
guileless, profound, confident, and trustful. She carried her
sorrowful head as though she were proud of that sorrow, as
though she would say, I – I alone know how to mourn for him as
he deserves. But while we were still shaking hands, such a look of

awful desolation came upon her face that I perceived she was one of those creatures that are not the playthings of Time. For her he had died only yesterday. And, by Jove! the impression was so powerful that for me too he seemed to have died only yesterday — nay, this very minute. I saw her and him in the same instant of time — his death and her sorrow. I saw her sorrow in the very moment of his death. It was too terrible. Do you understand? I saw them together — I heard them together. She had said, with a deep catch of the breath, "I have survived"; while my strained ears seemed to hear distinctly, mingled with her tone of despairing regret, the summing-up whisper of his eternal condemnation. I tell you it was terrible. I asked myself what I was doing there, with a sensation of panic in my heart as though I had blundered into a place of cruel and absurd mysteries not fit for a human being to behold. I wanted to get out. She motioned me to a chair. We sat down. I laid the packet gently on the little table, and she put her hand over it. "You knew him well," she murmured, after a moment of mourning silence.

'"Intimacy grows quick out there," I said. "I knew him as well as it is possible for one man to know another."

'"And you admired him," she said. "It was impossible to know him and not to admire him. Was it?"

'"He was a remarkable man," I said, unsteadily. Then before the appealing fixity of her gaze, that seemed to watch for more words on my lips, I went on, "It was impossible not to —"

'"Love him," she finished eagerly, silencing me into an appalled dumbness. "How true! how true! But when you think that no one knew him so well as I! I had all his noble confidence. I knew him best."

'"You knew him best," I repeated. And perhaps she did. But I fancied that with every word spoken the room was growing darker, and only her forehead, smooth and white, remained illumined by the unextinguishable light of belief and love.

'"You were his friend," she went on. "His friend," she repeated, a little louder. "You must have been, if he had given this to you, and sent you to me. I feel I can speak to you — oh, I must speak. I want you — you who have heard his last words — to know I

have been worthy of him . . . It is not pride . . . Yes! I am proud to
know I understood him better than any one on earth – he said so
himself. And since his mother died I have had no one – no one – to
– to —"

'I listened. The darkness deepened. I was not even sure whether
he had given me the right bundle. I rather suspect he wanted me to
take care of another batch of his papers which, after his death, I
saw the manager examining under the lamp. But in the box I had
brought to his bedside there were several packages pretty well
alike, all tied with shoe-strings, and probably he had made a
mistake. And the girl talked, easing her pain in the certitude of my
sympathy; she talked as thirsty men drink. I had heard that her
engagement with Kurtz had been disapproved generally. He
wasn't rich enough or something. And indeed I don't know
whether he had not been a pauper all his life. He had given me
some reason to infer that it was his impatience of comparative
poverty that drove him out there.

' ". . . Who was not his friend who had heard him speak once?"
she was saying. "He drew men towards him by what was best in
them." She looked at me with intensity. "It is the gift of the great,"
she went on, and the sound of her low voice seemed to have the
accompaniment of all the other sounds, full of mystery, desolation, and sorrow, I had ever heard – the ripple of the river, the
soughing of the trees swayed by the wind, the murmurs of wild
crowds, the faint ring of incomprehensible words cried from afar,
the whisper of a voice speaking from beyond the threshold of an
eternal darkness. "But you have heard him! You know!" she
cried.

' "Yes, I know," I said with something like despair in my heart,
but bowing my head before the faith that was in her, before that
great and saving illusion that shone with an unearthly glow in the
darkness, in the triumphant darkness from which I could not have
defended her – from which I could not even defend myself.

' "What a loss to me – to us!" – she corrected herself with
beautiful generosity; then added in a murmur, "To the world." By
the last gleams of twilight I could see the glitter of her eyes, full of
tears – of tears that would not fall.

‘ "I have been very happy – very fortunate – very proud," she went on. "Too fortunate. Too happy for a little while. And now I am unhappy for – for life."

'She stood up; her fair hair seemed to catch all the remaining light in a glimmer of gold. I rose too.

‘ "And of all this," she went on, mournfully, "of all his promise, and of all his greatness, of his generous mind, of his noble heart, nothing remains – nothing but a memory. You and I —"

‘ "We shall always remember him," I said, hastily.

‘ "No!" she cried. "It is impossible that all this should be lost – that such a life should be sacrificed to leave nothing – but sorrow. You know he had vast plans. I knew them too – I could not perhaps understand, – but others knew of them. Something must remain. His words, at least, have not died."

‘ "His words will remain," I said.

‘ "And his example," she whispered to herself. "Wherever he went men looked up to him, – his goodness shone in every act. His example —"

‘ "True," I said; "his example too. Yes, his example. I forgot that."

‘ "But I do not. I cannot – I cannot believe – not yet. I cannot believe that I shall never see him again, that nobody will ever see him again, never, never, never."

'She put out her arms as if after a retreating figure, stretching them black and with clasped pale hands across the fading and narrow sheen of the window. Never see him. I saw him clearly enough then. I shall see this eloquent phantom as long as I live, and I shall see her too, a tragic and familiar Shade, resembling in this gesture another one, tragic also, and bedecked with powerless charms, stretching bare brown arms over the glitter of the infernal stream, the stream of darkness.* She said suddenly very low, "He died as he lived."

‘ "His end," said I, with dull anger stirring in me, "was in every way worthy of his life."

‘ "And I was not with him," she murmured. My anger subsided before a feeling of infinite pity.

‘ "Everything that could be done —" I mumbled.

' "Ah, but I believed in him more than any one on earth – more than his own mother, more than – himself. He needed me! Me! I would have treasured every sigh, every murmur, every word, every sign, every glance."

'I felt like a chill grip on my chest. "Don't," I said, in a muffled voice.

' "Forgive me. I – I – have mourned so long in silence – in silence . . . You were with him – to the last? I think of his loneliness. Nobody near to understand him as I would have understood. Perhaps no one to hear . . ."

' "To the very end," I said, shakily. "I heard his very last words . . ." I stopped in a fright.

' "Repeat them," she said in a heart-broken tone. "I want – I want – something – something – to – to live with."

'I was on the point of crying at her, "Don't you hear them?" The dusk was repeating them in a persistent whisper all around us, in a whisper that seemed to swell menacingly like the first whisper of a rising wind. "The horror! the horror!"

' "His last word – to live with," she murmured. "Don't you understand I loved him – I loved him – I loved him!"

'I pulled myself together and spoke slowly.

' "The last word he pronounced was – your name."

'I heard a light sigh, and then my heart stood still, stopped dead short by an exulting and terrible cry, by the cry of inconceivable triumph and of unspeakable pain. "I knew it – I was sure!" She knew. She was sure. I heard her weeping, her face in her hands. It seemed to me that the house would collapse before I could escape, that the heavens would fall upon my head. But nothing happened. The heavens do not fall for such a trifle. Would they have fallen, I wonder, if I had rendered Kurtz that justice which was his due? Hadn't he said he wanted only justice?* But I couldn't. I could not tell her. It would have been too dark – too dark altogether . . .'

Marlow ceased, and sat apart, indistinct and silent, in the pose of a meditating Buddha. Nobody moved for a time. 'We have lost the first of the ebb,' said the Director, suddenly. I looked around. The offing was barred by a black bank of clouds, and the tranquil waterway leading to the uttermost ends of the earth flowed sombre under an overcast sky – seemed to lead also into the heart of an immense darkness.

NOTES

(Place-names and nautical terms are listed in the Glossary.)

Key to Abbreviations:

CLJC: *The Collected Letters of Joseph Conrad*, ed. Frederick R. Karl and Laurence Davies (Cambridge: Cambridge University Press; Vol. 1, 1983; Vol. 2, 1986; Vol. 3, 1988; Vol. 4, 1990).

CWW: Norman Sherry: *Conrad's Western World* (London: Cambridge University Press, 1971).

Hawkins: Hunt Hawkins: 'Conrad's Critique of Imperialism in *Heart of Darkness*': PMLA, 94 (1979), pp. 286–99.

JCC: Zdzisław Najder: *Joseph Conrad: A Chronicle* (Cambridge: Cambridge University Press, 1983).

Kimbrough: Joseph Conrad: *Heart of Darkness*, ed. Robert Kimbrough (3rd edn: New York and London: Norton, 1988).

KLC: Ruth Slade: *King Leopold's Congo* (London: Oxford University Press, 1962).

LE: Joseph Conrad: *Last Essays* [1926] (London: Dent, 1955).

LP: Guy Burrows: *The Land of the Pigmies* (London: Burrows, 1898).

MA: Alfred Russel Wallace: *The Malay Archipelago* [1869] (London: Macmillan, 1890).

MS: Joseph Conrad: *The Mirror of the Sea* [1906] (London: Dent, 1946).

PR: Joseph Conrad: *A Personal Record* [1912] (London: Dent, 1946).

Youth: Joseph Conrad: *Youth: A Narrative / and / Two Other Stories* (Edinburgh and London: Blackwood, 1902).

p. 1 The Heart of Darkness: the title is richly ambiguous. 'The heart of darkness' could mean the centre of a dark (obscure, mysterious, sinister or evil) place. In the tale, it is applied to central Africa, but London is described as the centre of 'brooding gloom'. The phrase could also mean 'The person's heart which is dark' (obscure, mysterious, sinister or evil), and thus anticipates the depiction of Kurtz. Darkness also connotes in the tale: the death of the individual or of the human race; 'dark ages' between periods of civilisation; the abominable; the primordial; the inscrutable; the unknown; the mapped. Light is associated with civilisation and truth but also with the brightness and destructiveness of fire. Whiteness is associated with hypocrisy, ivory, bones, death, fog and the unmapped. The title thus aptly introduces the ambiguities, paradoxes and enigmas of the tale.

When the work was reprinted, Conrad omitted the definite article from the title. This change strengthens the ambiguity: it seems to bring the sense of reference to a person into equipoise with the previously dominant sense of reference to a location.

p. 3 *Nellie* ..... rest: G. F. W. Hope, a company director, owned the yawl *Nellie*, and made sailing expeditions with his friends E. G. Mears (a commercial clerk), W. B. Keen (an accountant), and Conrad.

p. 3 I have already said somewhere: the 'somewhere' is paragraph two of the tale 'Youth', which had been published in *Blackwood's Magazine* in September 1898 (only five months before the serialisation of 'The Heart of Darkness' commenced in the same magazine).

p. 3 bones: at that time dominoes were often made of ivory (and were therefore white with black spots). The reference serves to link this British accountant to the other accountant who, in Africa, remorselessly serves the ivory-trade.

p. 5 that never returned: Sir Francis Drake (*c.* 1540–96) was knighted by Queen Elizabeth I at Deptford aboard *The Golden Hind*, the ship in which he had circumnavigated the globe and harried the Spaniards, returning with pillaged wealth. Sir John Franklin (1786–1847) commanded an expedition to find a north-west passage linking the North Atlantic to the North Pacific. Both its ships, *Erebus* and *Terror*, became ice-bound in the Arctic, and all the men died. See also 'Geography and Some Explorers' (*LE*), pp. 10–11.

p. 5 'interlopers' ..... fleets: 'interlopers' were traders who breached a legal monopoly. Brian Gardner's *The East India Company* (London: Hart-Davis, 1971), p. 50, says:

Another bane of the [East India] Company was the activity of the merchant interlopers ..... [I]n 1685 the Company mounted 48 prosecutions for interloping. In 1701, the notorious Captain Kidd was executed for piracy in the Indian Ocean .....

The 'commissioned "Generals" of East India fleets' were the commanders of the company's fleets: James Lancaster, for instance, was termed 'our Generall' (Gardner, p. 26).

The East India Company, originally chartered by Queen Elizabeth I in 1600, gradually took control of most of the Indian sub-continent until, in 1857–8, its authority there was transferred to the British government.

p. 5 dark places of the earth: Psalms 74:20. William Booth, in *In Darkest England and the Way Out* (London: Salvation Army, 1890), p. 11, said: 'As there is a darkest Africa is there not also a darkest England?'

p. 6 when the Romans first came here: Conrad's friend R. B. Cunninghame Graham, in his *Notes on the District of Menteith* (London: Black, 1895), p. 81, wrote:

History informs us that the Romans once ruled the greater part of Scotland .....
  What an abode of horror it must have been to the unfortunate centurion, say from Naples, stranded in a marsh far from the world, in a climate of the roughest, and blocked on every side by painted savages!

p. 6 you say Knights?: this interjection retrospectively modifies the status of the anonymous narrator's reflections on the Thames and her 'knights all, titled and untitled'. Evidently the statements from 'The tidal current' to 'germs of empires' should be regarded as tacitly-reported speech, representing words originally uttered aloud. Hence the shift to the pluperfect tense during that descriptive passage.

p. 6 what we read: Julius Caesar's *De Bello Gallico*, V, 1–2, claims that the Romans preparing to invade Britain constructed 628 ships in one winter.

p. 5 mend his fortunes: in this finely proleptic paragraph, the account of the 'trireme commander' partly anticipates the description of Marlow's experiences, while the account of this 'decent young citizen' partly anticipates what will be said of Kurtz. Section XXX of Conrad's *The Mirror of the Sea* (1906) again imagines a Roman galley-commander's first voyage up the Thames (*MS*, pp. 101–2).

p. 7 without a lotus-flower: Buddhist scriptures confer many symbolic meanings on the lotus-flower: these include 'enlightening doctrine', 'spiritual grace', 'paradisal beauty', 'purity' and 'the support and ground of manifestation'. In paintings and sculptures of Buddha, a cross-legged posture indicates meditation or preaching; a raised fore-arm with palm outwards usually signifies reassurance. The linkage of Marlow and Buddha is partly superficial, a mere visual coincidence of posture and gesture; it is partly ironic, for Marlow is a western sceptic; and partly substantial, for, like Buddha, he imparts wisdom by means of puzzling paradoxes which emphasise the snares of desire (and of language) and sometimes suggest the impermanence or even illusoriness of the familiar world.

p. 7 efficiency: 'efficiency' was a quality highly commended in the 1890s by Social Darwinists, Liberal imperialists and Fabian imperialists. In 1901 Conrad said that *The Inheritors* (which he co-authored with F. M. Hueffer) attacked the fasionable 'worship' of 'unscrupulous efficiency' (*CLJC*, 2, p. 348).

p. 7 what was to be got: in the manuscript, this sentence was followed by a passage contrasting the Romans favourably with the modern Belgians: at least the Romans did not have 'an association on a philanthropic basis to develop Britain, with some third rate king for a president' (Kimbrough, p. 10).

p. 7 Flames . . . . . separating slowly or hastily: the 'flames' are the lights of vessels, and their reflections in the water. A sailing vessel carried a green light on the starboard side and a red light on the port side. Steamers carried, in addition, a white light on or in front of the foremast.

p. 7 sleepless river: in the manuscript there followed a passage which, after describing a big steamer 'bound to the uttermost ends of earth', concluded by likening the earth to a pea 'spinning in the heart of an immense darkness' (Kimbrough, p. 11). These omitted lines thus anticipated the phrasing of the tale's final paragraph.

p. 8 I will go there: Marlow's recollections resemble Conrad's, as given in *PR*, p. 13:

> It was in 1868, when nine years old or thereabouts, that while looking at a map of Africa of the time and putting my finger on the blank space then representing the unsolved mystery of that continent, I said to myself with absolute assurance and an amazing audacity which are no longer in my character now:
> 'When I grow up I shall go *there*.'

There is a similar passage in 'Geography and Some Explorers' (*LE*), p. 16.

p. 9 dream gloriously over: in 'Geography and Some Explorers' (*LE*),

p. 14, Conrad recalls that in his childhood atlas, printed in 1852, 'The heart of its Africa was white and big'. The explorations of Sir Richard Burton and Captain J. H. Speke then helped to fill such space with details of the interior of the continent.

p. 9 a Company for trade on that river: the river is evidently the Congo, and the company corresponds to the Société Anonyme Belge pour le Commerce du Haut-Congo (the Belgian Limited Company for Trade on the Upper Congo), which had its headquarters at Brussels.

p. 9 enthusiastic soul: she is based partly on Marguerite Poradowska, whom Conrad addressed as 'Aunt' (though she was really the wife of a remote cousin) and who lived in Brussels. In November 1889 Conrad was interviewed in that city by Captain Albert Thys, director of the Société Anonyme Belge, and was promised the command of a paddle-steamer in the Congo. In February 1890, around the time of her husband's death, Conrad visited Madame Poradowska; he was again interviewed, but doubted the outcome; yet, in April, the appointment was confirmed. Apparently she had exerted her influence on Conrad's behalf. (Her friends included A. J. Wauters, secretary-general of the Compagnies Belges du Congo.)

p. 10 Fresleven: Otto Lütken, in 'Joseph Conrad in the Congo' (*London Mercury*, 22 [May 1930], p. 43), states:

> [Johannes] Frieisleben, a Danish captain, and Conrad's predecessor in com-
> mand of the *Florida*, was killed by the natives at Tchumbei [actually Tchumbiri]
> in some dispute over firewood or fresh provisions; but his bones were recovered
> on the 24th March, 1890[,] by the two steamers . . . . . The steamers had
> soldiers on board and some Belgian officers . . . . . ; and there was a good deal of
> shooting and burning of native huts . . . . . Duhst, who *was* there, tells of the
> grass growing through the bones of the skeleton which lay where it had fallen.

p. 10 whited sepulchre: according to St Matthew's gospel (23:27–8), Jesus said:

> Woe unto you, scribes and Pharisees, hypocrites! for ye are like unto whited
> sepulchres, which indeed appear beautiful outward, but are within full of dead
> *men's* bones, and of all uncleanness.
> Even so ye also outwardly appear righteous unto men, but within ye are full of
> hypocrisy and iniquity.

Marlow associates Brussels with hypocrisy because of the 'philanthropic pretence' masking the desire to 'make no end of coin by trade'.

Hans van Marle suggests privately that 'the Brussels Palais de Justice in its nineteenth-century whiteness towering on top of a hill above the old city has contributed to the image' of the whited sepulchre.

p. 11 **Two women . . . . . knitting black wool:** In this paragraph Conrad anticipates Kafka: the realism has qualities of the dreamlike and the elusively symbolic. The knitting women are credibly bored functionaries; they also prompt legendary and literary associations. In the Greek legend of the three Fates, Clotho and Lachesis spin the thread of each life before Atropos cuts it. In Virgil's *Aeneid*, the wise Sibyl guards the door of the Underworld into which Aeneas will venture. Charles Dickens's *A Tale of Two Cities* describes Madame Defarge, who knits 'with the steadfastness of Fate'; she says she is knitting shrouds; her companion in the task is called 'Vengeance'; and the knitwork incorporates the names of the exploiters who are to incur retribution.

p. 11 **real work is done in there:** nevertheless, Kurtz is partly a product of England, as the narrative will later emphasise.

p. 11 **yellow:** British late-nineteenth-century maps of the world often coloured British territories red, French territories blue, Italian green, Portuguese orange, German purple, and Belgian yellow. (Tanganyika, on the east coast of Africa, became a German protectorate in 1891.)

p. 11 **pale plumpness in a frock-coat:** doubtless a recollection of Captain Albert Thys, the director who had interviewed Conrad. (In photographs taken between 1887 and 1892 he is markedly plump.)

p. 12 **trade secrets:** cf. 'I am destined for the command of a steamboat . . . . . but I know nothing for certain as everything is supposed to be kept secret' (Conrad to Karol Zagórski, 22 May 1890: *CLJC*, 1, p. 52).

p. 12 ***Ave!* . . . . . *Morituri te salutant*:** the original Latin form was 'Ave Cæsar [*or* Ave imperator], morituri te salutant': 'Hail, Cæsar [*or* Hail, emperor]; those about to die salute you': the gladiators' salutation on entering the arena of combat.

p. 12 **assured me the secretary:** one of Conrad's lapses into French word-order.

p. 13 **measure my head:** the doctor is a craniologist and craniometrist: he measures the cranium in order to compare and classify the characteristics of different individuals and races. A. R. Wallace's *The Malay Archipelago*, one of Conrad's favourite books, postulated a correlation between (a) different races' average cranial size and skull-capacity and (b) 'their mental activity and capacity for civilization' (*MA*, pp. 459–62). In 1881 Dr Izydor Kopernicki, a Polish anthropologist, had asked Conrad to assist his craniological studies by collecting skulls of natives and dispatching them to Kraków.

p. 14 Workers, with a capital – you know: cf. Thomas Carlyle, *Past and Present* [1843] (London: Chapman & Hall, 1858), p. 302:

> But it is to you, ye Workers, ... that the whole world calls for new work and nobleness. Subdue mutiny, discord, widespread despair, by manfulness, justice, mercy and wisdom. Chaos is dark, deep as Hell; let light be, and there is instead a green flowery World . . . . . It is work for a God. Sooty Hell of mutiny and savagery and despair can, by man's energy, be made a kind of Heaven . . . . .

This was the passage that H. M. Stanley quoted in 1898 when suggesting that 'God chose the King [Leopold II] for his instrument' to redeem the Congo (Kimbrough, p. 79).

p. 14 rot let loose . . . . . time: in 1889, for example, Leopold II opened the international 'Brussels Conference for the Abolition of the Slave-Trade', which was widely publicised; and Albert Thys published his proposals for the Lower Congo railway, concluding:

> We must also appeal to philanthropists and men of goodwill who are horrified by the barbarities of the slave-trade; . . . . . to religious and believing men who suffer to see the unfortunate blacks held in the ignorance of fetish-worship. All these friends of humanity will find that the Congo railway is the means *par excellence* of allowing civilisation to penetrate rapidly and surely into the unknown depths of Africa.
>
> (Quoted in *KLC*, p. 75.)

p. 14 the labourer is worthy of his hire . . . . . : Luke 10:7. Jesus explains that the diligent disciples are entitled to accept hospitable donations during their missionary journeys.

p. 14 It's queer . . . . . whole thing over: in *Chance* (London: Methuen, 1914), p. 131, Marlow says the opposite:

> 'The women's rougher, simpler, more upright judgment, embraces the whole truth, which their tact, their mistrust of masculine idealism, ever prevents them from speaking in its entirety . . . . . We could not stand women speaking the truth . . . . . It would cause infinite misery and bring about most awful disturbances in this rather mediocre, but still idealistic fool's paradise in which each of us lives his own little life . . . . .'

p. 15 Gran' Bassam, Little Popo . . . . . : in 1890, when Conrad voyaged from Bordeaux to the mouth of the Congo in the steamer *Ville de Maceio*, the vessel called at Grand Bassam (or Bassa) on the Ivory Coast and

Grand Popo in Dahomey, now Benin (*CWW*, p. 23). Little Popo (or Anecho) is in Togo, formerly Togoland.

p. 16 wars going on thereabouts: Conrad later explained (*CLJC*, 3, p. 94):

> If I say that the ship which bombarded the coast was French, it was quite simply because *it was* a French ship. I recall its name – the *Seignelay*. It was during the war(!) with Dahomey.

Between February and October 1890, the French attempted to conquer the African kingdom of Dahomey by bombardment and invasion.

p. 16 seat of the government: Conrad stayed one night at Boma, the 'seat of government' for the Congo Free State. In the manuscript of 'The Heart of Darkness', Conrad writes scornfully of the place, particularly its 'greasy and dingy' hotel. Sherry (*CWW*, p. 27) says that in 1890 Boma, with its steam-tramway, hotel and post office, was actually 'a well-established, well-organised seat of government'. He suggests that Marlow repeatedly understates the organised extent of colonisation, trade and communications in central Africa. Marlow, however, chooses not to specify the dates of his journey.

p. 18 building a railway: construction of the 270-mile railway-line from Matadi to Kinshasa was beset by difficulties, and it took eight years instead of the estimated four. Trans-shipment of freight from large vessels to small at Boma often resulted in breakages. (Hawkins, p. 290.)

p. 18 unhappy savages: 'On 9 August 1890, a royal decree [by Leopold II] permitted the railway company to establish a militia to impress workers from the surrounding area' (Hawkins, p. 292). Forced labour, under various pretexts, became widespread in the Congo.

p. 19 circle of some Inferno: Marlow's journey has intermittent (though distant) analogies with Dante's journey into hell: he sees suffering and tormented beings, learns of various kinds of corruption, and, on meeting Kurtz, encounters a flagrant malefactor.

p. 19 helpers had withdrawn to die: Louis Goffin's *Le Chemin de fer du Congo* (Brussels: Weissenbruch, 1907), pp. 43–4, notes the high mortality-rate among the African workers during the construction of the railway in the Lower Congo. In one month of 1891, for example, 150 men (nearly 8 per cent of the work force) perished. Goffin remarks that they often withdrew into the bush to die. Numerous Europeans either died or (like Conrad in December 1890) were sent home suffering from tropical diseases.

On the other hand, Conrad's diary (*LE*, pp. 161–2) gives no indication that he saw any 'grove of death' at Matadi (which corresponds geographically to this fictional outer station). His stay there was partly tedious, with 'people speaking ill of each other', but partly pleasant; he greatly enjoyed meeting Roger Casement, and found Mr Underwood 'hearty and kind'. (Casement later became a leading campaigner against harsh exploitation in the Congo and in the Putumayo region of South America.)

p. 19 time contracts: G. W. Williams, who traversed the Congo in 1890, reported that labourers were often recruited from distant coastal regions and were expected to work for one year (Kimbrough, pp. 95, 106).

p. 22 Kurtz: in the manuscript, Conrad initially used the name 'Klein' before changing it to 'Kurtz'. When Conrad, in the *Roi des Belges*, reached Stanley Falls in September 1890, the vessel took on board an agent of the company, Georges Antoine Klein. The agent was suffering from dysentery, and died while the paddle-steamer was making her way downstream. 'Klein' is German for 'small'; 'kurz' (pronounced 'koorts') is German for 'short'. Marlow later explains the doubly ironic significance of Kurtz's name.

p. 22 two-hundred-mile tramp: this part of Marlow's journey corresponds geographically to Conrad's overland trek from Matadi to Kinshasa between June and August 1890. Sherry (*CWW*, pp. 38–9) notes that whereas Marlow describes a depopulated region, 'Conrad's journey took him to many market places, to various stations, and he passed *en route* other caravans'. Nevertheless, G. W. Williams reported in 1890 that many inhabitants had moved away or been killed 'by war or small pox epidemic' (Kimbrough, p. 93), and E. D. Morel lists areas depopulated after raids and outrages by the State soldiers (*Red Rubber* [London: Unwin, 1906], pp. 44–6).

p. 23 Zanzibaris: the soldiers in the Congo were 'very largely imported from Zanzibar' (G. W. Williams: Kimbrough, p. 106).

p. 23 bullet-hole in the forehead: Conrad's diary of the trek from Matadi to Kinshasa (*LE*, pp. 161–71) includes the following items:

Met an off[icer] of the State inspecting. A few minutes afterwards saw at a camp[ing] place the dead body of a Backongo. Shot? Horrid smell . . . . .

Saw another dead body lying by the path in an attitude of meditative repose . . . . .

On the road to-day passed a skeleton tied up to a post . . . . .

Chief came with a youth about 13 suffering from gun-shot wound in the head . . . . .

p. 23 rows with the carriers: On Conrad's trek, his European companion, Prosper Harou, became very ill with fever and had to be carried in a hammock by the African porters. He was heavy, and quarrels ensued. (*LE*, pp. 169–70.)

p. 24 the real significance of that wreck . . . . . : when Conrad reached Kinshasa early in August 1890, he found that the steamer *Florida*, which he had expected to command, was wrecked. In the tale, Conrad has converted this fact into part of a 'covert plot'. The 'real significance' of the fictional wreck is the probability that the central station's manager arranged for the 'mishap' to occur. The manager hopes to destroy Kurtz, his main rival for promotion, by delaying the relief of the inner station until Kurtz has become mortally ill. After the steamer has been wrecked, the manager then impedes the repairs for three months by intercepting Marlow's requests for rivets. By the time the vessel reaches its goal, Kurtz (who has thus been isolated for well over a year) is dying.

Sherry (*CWW*, pp.44–7) says that Conrad had taken an exceptionally long time to trek from Matadi to Kinshasa (35 days instead of the usual 17–20), and might well have been reproached for tardiness. If so, the tale imaginatively transfers culpability from Conrad to the manager.

p. 25 nor even respect: while staying at Kinshasa, Conrad wrote to Marguerite Poradowska (*CLJC*, 1, p. 62):

From the manager in Africa who has taken the trouble to tell one and all that I offend him supremely, down to the lowest mechanic, they all have the gift of irritating my nerves – so that I am not as agreeable to them perhaps as I should be. The manager is a common ivory dealer with base instincts who considers himself a merchant though he is only a kind of African shop-keeper. His name is Delcommune.

This was Camille Delcommune (1859–92), manager of the Société Belge du Haut-Congo.

p. 26 no entrails: Arthur Hodister, trader in the Congo, allegedly had 'no heart and no entrails' (*CWW*, pp. 114–15).

p. 28 'take advantage of this unfortunate accident': presumably by using the destruction of the shed containing trading goods as another pretext for delaying Kurtz's relief – though the pretext is not needed. (At Kinshasa in 1890 a fire destroyed much merchandise: *CWW*, p. 42.)

p. 28 straw maybe: Exodus 5: 6–19 tells how the Israelites, denied straw by Pharaoh, were consequently unable to make bricks. Sherry (*CWW*, pp. 43–4) notes that the brick-maker at Kinshasa in 1890 was 'singularly active' in organising the production of many bricks.

p. 28 An act of special creation perhaps: a mocking allusion to those who, in the nineteenth-century controversy about evolutionary theories, maintained that God directly operated as creator.

p. 29 percentages: agents were paid a commission on ivory which rose in inverse proportion to the sums they paid for it. 'The less the native got . . . . . , the larger the Official's commission!' (Morel, *Red Rubber*, p. 32.)

p. 29 look at a halter: as 'halter' means (here) 'rope or strap for leading a horse', Marlow is offering a witty variant of the old proverb, 'One man may steal a horse, while another may not look over a hedge' (meaning that some people commit crimes with impunity, while others are punished for trivial or imaginary misdemeanours).

p. 29 His allusions were Chinese to me: the 1902 text omits this sentence.

p. 29 a woman, draped and blindfolded, carrying a lighted torch: Astræa, goddess of justice, is often depicted as blindfolded (meaning that ideal justice is impartial), and Liberty is famously depicted as brandishing a lighted torch; but Kurtz has created a new and highly ironic symbol. From his viewpoint, the painting presumably expresses the idea that the advance of civilisation into the darkness of Africa lacks vision (hence the blindfold); his idealistic writings were designed to provide that vision. Marlow has sarcastically referred to Roman colonists as 'men going at it blind – as is very proper for those who tackle a darkness'. The primary narrator had described British adventurers positively as bearers of 'the torch', 'bearers of a spark from the sacred fire'. Conrad, however, provides many suggestions that the burning torch is an ambiguous symbol, for it may be destructive (starting conflagrations) rather than illuminative: hence, perhaps, the 'sinister' effect of the torch-light on the bearer's face. And what makes the picture so fully symbolic is the fact that, though it solicits decipherment, it retains a residue of the indeterminable.

p. 30 devil knows what else: Sherry (*CWW*, pp. 95–118) suggests that Kurtz is based partly on Arthur Hodister, an ambitious, successful and idealistic ivory-collector.

p. 31 papier-mâché Mephistopheles: papier-mâché is paper (or paper-pulp) treated to make such items as trays, boxes and light furniture, or imitation plaster moulding; it is cheap, deceptive and lacks strength. Hence, 'if I tried I could poke my forefinger through him'. Mephistopheles, who is prominent in Marlowe's and Goethe's versions of the Faust legend, is the diabolic agent of Lucifer.

p. 32 We live, as we dream – alone . . . . . : Conrad sometimes quoted Calderón's maxim, 'La vida es sueño' ('Life is a dream'); and Decoud, in *Nostromo* (1904), remarks: 'All this is life, must be life, since it is so much like a dream.' Among writers whose works were studied by Conrad, Schopenhauer quoted Calderón's phrase and emphasised 'the frailty, vanity and dream-like quality of all things', Maupassant repeatedly voiced the fear of utter solitude, and Walter Pater (in *Marius the Epicurean*) let Marius reflect:

> the ideas we are somehow impelled to form of an outer world, and of other minds akin to our own, are, it may be, but a day-dream . . . . .

Marlow's words 'We live . . . . . alone' constitute an oxymoron, for the solipsism of 'alone' is contradicted by the generality of 'we'.

p. 34 hippopotamus: the connection between the hippopotamus and the rivets is soon implied. Whereas the hippopotamus 'has a charmed life', 'no man here bears a charmed life'. Kurtz is vulnerable, and the manager is increasing his vulnerability by protracting the steamer's repair. The brick-maker's remark, 'I write from dictation', implies that the manager has prevented the transmission of Marlow's request for rivets; and, since the brick-maker 'had been planning to be assistant-manager by-and-by under the present man', his loyalty is to the manager rather than to Kurtz. Marlow fails to perceive the brick-maker's logic, and therefore wrongly assumes that he has persuaded the man to transmit the request: hence his subsequent assurance to the boiler-maker – 'We shall have rivets!'

p. 36 the uncle . . . . . was leader of that lot: one source for this character was Alexandre Delcommune, elder brother of Camille Delcommune, and leader of an expedition into mineral-rich Katanga (*CWW*, pp. 83–6).

p. 38 hanged! Why not?: in 1895 a Belgian officer in the Congo arrested and hanged on the spot a British lay-missionary, Charlie Stokes, who had sold arms to Arabs. The British government protested, but the officer was acquitted. (Neal Ascherson, *The King Incorporated* [London: Allen & Unwin, 1963], p. 243.) Conrad may have read about this incident.

p. 39 Conceive you – that ass!: 'Conceive you' is a Conradian Gallicism (recalling 'concevez-vous' or 'conçois-tu'); the meaning is 'Can you imagine?'. Another Gallicism, a few lines above, is 'I did my possible'. Other instances are: 'Famous' (for 'Splendid', p. 13); 'you conceive' (p. 33); 'My faith' (p. 64); and 'I felt like a chill grip on my chest' (p. 95).

p. 40 fate of the less valuable animals: in 1890 the Delcommune expedition (with more than 150 soldiers) proceeded by steamboat to Bena-Kamba, its progress being reported in the weekly *Mouvement Géographique*, published in Brussels (*CWW*, pp. 84–5).

p. 40 alligators: 'crocodiles' is the usual term for these African reptiles.

p. 41 next day's steaming: when Conrad voyaged up the Congo from Kinshasa to Stanley Falls in the *Roi des Belges*, the captain was Ludwig Koch, and Conrad made navigational notes in preparation for the time when (he expected) he himself would be captain of one of the company's vessels. The *Roi des Belges*, a paddle-steamer fuelled by timber, closely resembled the vessel described in the tale; and Conrad's notes make evident the dangers presented by snags, stones and sandbanks in the river. Sherry (*CWW*, pp. 48–61) suggests various differences between the fictional journey and the biographical facts: in particular, the original voyage was 'a routine, highly organised venture along a fairly frequented riverway linking quite numerous settlements of trading posts and factories'. Najder, however, disputes this, citing a traveller's report that on a 200-mile stretch of the Congo 'there is not an inhabited village left' in 'a country formerly so rich, today entirely ruined' (*JCC*, pp. 134–5).

p. 41 cannibals . . . . . : S. L. Hinde, who travelled on the Congo at this period, reported (*LP*, p. 142):

> When I was returning from Stanley Falls on my homeward journey six of the [Bangala] crew were in irons on board ship, whom the captain delivered up to justice at Bangala for having eaten two of their number during the voyage up to the falls.

Norman Sherry (*CWW*, pp. 59–60) comments:

The crews of steamers were from the upper Congo, mostly from Bangala . . . . .
Like Marlow's cannibal crew, the Bangalas were joyfully cannibalistic. The
brother of Bapulula (popular pilot on the mission steamer *Peace* on the river at
this time), when asked if he ate human flesh, answered, 'Ah! I wish I could eat
everybody on earth'. Dr Bentley, the missionary, recalls talking to an old man at
Bangala, three years before Conrad went up the river, who was reported to have
killed and eaten seven of his wives.

G. W. Williams reported in 1890 that some of the soldiers in the Congo
were 'bloodthirsty cannibalistic Bangalas' who ate the bodies of slain
children (Kimbrough, p. 110).

p. 43 Principles . . . . . rags . . . . . shake: Marlow had read Carlyle's
Sartor Resartus (mentioned in *Youth*), which likens ideology to
clothing, declaring that 'the solemnities and paraphernalia of civilised
Life, which we make so much of, [are] nothing but so many Cloth-
rags . . . . .' (London: Chapman & Hall, 1891, p. 44).

p. 44 terrible vengeance: cf. Azuma-zi's awed service of the big dynamo
in H. G. Wells's tale 'Lord of the Dynamos' (1894).

p. 45 Tower, Towson . . . . . Navy: J. A. Arnold, in *Conradiana*, 7
(1976), pp. 121–6, suggests that Marlow or Conrad linked the name of
J. T. Towson to a book by Nicholas Tinmouth. Towson published
navigational tables but not a handbook, whereas Tinmouth published in
1845 *An Inquiry Relative to Various Important Points of Seamanship,
Considered as a Branch of Practical Science*. Its preface manifests both
the humility and the 'concern for the right way of going to work' that
Marlow notes; and the subsequent chapters, based on 'half-a-century' of
maritime experience, do indeed 'inquir[e] earnestly into the breaking
strain of ships' chains and tackle'. The book also includes eighteen of the
'illustrative diagrams' and three of the 'repulsive tables of figures'
mentioned by Marlow. Tinmouth, however, was not a 'Master in his
Majesty's Navy' but a Master-Attendant at Her Majesty's dock-yard at
Woolwich.

p. 49 brass wire . . . . . villages: J. Rose Troup, in *With Stanley's Rear
Column* (London: Chapman & Hall, 1890), pp. 103–4, states:

> The mitako, or brass rod, is the currency among the natives at Leopoldville and
> most of the regions of the Upper Congo. It is in general imported to the Congo
> by the State in large rolls or coils of 60 lbs. in weight. After its arrival at
> Leopoldville it is cut up into the regulation lengths (about 2 feet) . . . . . ; the
> value of each of these pieces at Leopoldville is reckoned at 1½d.

p. 49 stuff like half-cooked dough: kwanga, i.e. cassava (also known as manioc or tapioca), steeped and boiled to form a stiff dough; sometimes combined with ground millet and preservatives. It is indeed 'of a dirty lavender colour' but is long-lasting and sustaining.

p. 55 steam-whistle . . . . . screech hurriedly: Sherry (*CWW*, pp. 54–5) says that in relatively unexplored areas of the Congo, steam-whistles had been used by George Grenfell (1886) and H. M. Stanley (1887) to scatter hostile Africans. During Conrad's journey in 1890, however, the Africans living below Stanley Falls 'must have regarded both steamers and whistles as commonplace occurrences and are unlikely to have been affected by them'.

p. 57 cut up to the quick: corrected to 'cut to the quick' in the 1902 edition.

p. 58 They say the hair goes on growing sometimes: i.e. on corpses, Marlow having previously referred to 'the disinterred body of Mr Kurtz'. Subsequently Kurtz will be termed 'an initiated wraith', 'a shade' and a 'phantom'. Such imagery amplifies the Faustian plot-sequence concerning supernatural possession, according to which Kurtz has sold his soul to diabolical powers and is spiritually dead while yet inhabiting the world of the living. It is combined with suggestions of the vampiric. ('The thing was to know what he belonged to, how many powers of darkness claimed him for their own'; 'No fool ever made a bargain for his soul with the devil'; 'The wilderness had . . . . . sealed his soul to its own by the inconceivable ceremonies of some devilish initiation'; ' "I have been dead – and damned" '; 'More blood'.) The tale's imagery of the supernatural equivocates between the metaphoric and the literal; but, either way, the African 'wilderness' and some of its inhabitants are thus demonised.

p. 60 half-English . . . . . half-French: Conrad remarked: 'I took great care to give Kurtz a cosmopolitan origin' (*CLJC*, 3, p. 94).

p. 60 International Society for the Suppression of Savage Customs: Conrad was perhaps recalling the International Association for the Exploration and Civilising of Africa ('l'Association Internationale pour l'Exploration et la Civilisation en Afrique'), of which King Leopold II was the president, or the Anti-Slavery Society ('la Société Antiesclavagiste de Belgique'), with which Arthur Hodister was associated.

p. 60 unspeakable rites . . . . . himself: Norman Sherry notes that Arthur Hodister assisted at the fifteenth wedding of a chieftain, Tyabo, and witnessed human sacrifices decreed by Tyabo during funerary rites. In 1892 *The Times* reported that, during further explorations in the Congo, Hodister was captured and killed, his head stuck on a pole and his body eaten (*CWW*, pp. 95–118).

p. 65 **Van Shuyten:** 'impossible as a Dutch name; Van Schuyten will do', comments Hans van Marle.

p. 70 **heads on the stakes:** fifty-two human heads on stakes surrounded one station in the Congo where two white men stayed (*CWW*, pp. 117–18). E. J. Glave noted in 1895 that at Stanley Falls 'twenty-one heads . . . . . have been used by Captain Rom as a decoration round a flower-bed in front of his house' ('Cruelty in the Congo Free State': *Century Illustrated Monthly Magazine*, 54 [1897], p. 706).

p. 71 **hollow at the core:** the ancient proverb, 'The empty vessel makes the greatest sound' (Shakespeare: *Henry v*, IV.iv), partly explains Kurtz's combination of 'hollowness' and exceptional eloquence.

p. 85 **'Live rightly, die, die . . .':** in the manuscript of the tale, the phrase 'die nobly' completes the maxim (Kimbrough, p. 68).

p. 85 **a veil had been rent:** a remote echo of Luke 23:44–5: '[T]here was a darkness . . . . . , and the veil of the temple was rent . . . . .'

p. 85 **'The horror! The horror!':** different commentators interpret the cry in different ways; so does Marlow. He suggests the following meanings. (1) Kurtz condemns as horrible his corrupt actions, so that this 'judgment upon the adventures of his soul on this earth' is 'an affirmation, a moral victory'. (2) Kurtz deems hateful but also desirable the temptations to which he has succumbed: the whisper has 'the strange commingling of desire and hate'. (3) Kurtz deems horrible the inner natures of all mankind: 'no eloquence could have been so withering as his final burst of sincerity' when his stare 'penetrate[d] all the hearts that beat in the darkness'. (4) Kurtz deems horrible the whole universe: 'that wide and immense stare embracing, condemning, loathing all the universe . . . . . "The horror!"'

The cry thus serves as a thematic nexus, a climactic but highly ambiguous utterance which sums up, without resolving, several of the paradoxical themes of the tale. As is customary with symbols, the various meanings suggested do not exhaust the phrase's potential; it retains some opacity. Coordinated enigmas are a structural principle of 'The Heart of Darkness'.

p. 86 they very nearly buried me: Conrad, suffering from fever and dysentery, was allowed to return early from the Congo to Europe (*CWW*, p. 88; *JCC*, pp. 138–9).

p. 89 leader of an extreme party: Conrad knew the work of Max Nordau; and in Nordau's *Degeneration* (London: Heinemann, 1895), the description of the 'highly-gifted degenerate' (pp. 22–4) may have provided hints for the characterisation of Kurtz:

> 'The degenerate,' says Legrain, 'may be a genius. A badly balanced mind is susceptible of the highest conceptions, while, on the other hand, one meets in the same mind with traits of meanness and pettiness all the more striking from the fact that they co-exist with the most brilliant qualities.' . . . . . 'As regards their intellect, they can,' says Roubinovitch, 'attain to a high degree of development, but from a moral point of view their existence is completely deranged . . . A degenerate will employ his brilliant faculties quite as well in the service of some grand object as in the satisfaction of the basest propensities.' . . . . . I do not share Lombroso's opinion that highly gifted degenerates are an active force in the progress of mankind. They corrupt and delude; they do, alas! frequently exercise a deep influence, but this is always a baneful one . . . . . They, likewise, are leading men along the paths they themselves have found to new goals, but these goals are abysses or waste places. They are guides to swamps like will-o'-the-wisps, or to ruin like the ratcatcher of Hammelin.

p. 90 some other feeling perhaps: Conrad told David Meldrum that 'The Heart of Darkness' offered 'A mere shadow of love interest just in the last pages' (*CLJC*, 2, pp. 145–6).

p. 91 seemed to stare at me out of the gleaming panel: the memory of Kurtz's face perhaps suffuses the reflection of Marlow's in the panel; and the description may be influenced by the incident in Dickens's *A Christmas Carol* when Scrooge, about to open the door of his house, sees the staring face of the dead Marley, and associates it with a vision of horror:

> [T]hough the eyes were wide open, they were perfectly motionless. That, and its livid colour, made it horrible; but its horror seemed to be in spite of the face and beyond its control, rather than a part of its own expression.
>   (*Christmas Books* [London: Chapman & Hall, 1897], p. 19.)

p. 94 Shade . . . . . arms . . . . . darkness: Virgil's *Aeneid* (VI, 314) says that the Shades in the underworld 'stretched their arms out in longing' to Charon as they stood on the shore of Acheron, river of darkness.

p. 95 heavens would fall . . . . . justice?: Marlow is recalling the Latin maxim, 'Fiat iustitia ruat cælum [*or* cœlum]': 'Let justice be done, though the heavens fall'. Conrad quoted this as 'fiat justicia ruat cœlum' when writing to Marguerite Poradowska in March 1890, six weeks before setting out for the Congo (*CLJC*, 1, p. 43). The recurrence of this Latin tag is one of several features suggesting that the description of Marlow's meeting with the Intended is based, in part, on Conrad's relationship with 'Aunt' Marguerite in 1890. Marguerite, like Kurtz's fiancée, lived in Brussels. The fiancée is 'not very young'; Marguerite was 42. When Conrad visited Marguerite in April 1890 she, like the Intended, was bereaved and in mourning, for her husband had died in February. Marlow admires and is attracted to the Intended; Conrad admired and was attracted to Marguerite. Indeed, Conrad's uncle, Tadeusz Bobrowski, wrote to warn him against an infatuation which could not lead to marriage.

GLOSSARY

ALIENIST, *psychiatrist*
ALPACA *(p. 20), cloth made of wool from the South American animal, the alpaca*
ASSEGAI, *light spear*
AVE! . . . . . MORITURI TE SALUTANT, Hail! . . . . . Those about to die salute you

BEGGAR *(p. 62; slang), (mildly derogatory term for) fellow, person*
BLAMED *(p. 15), (euphemism for) blasted*
BON VOYAGE *(Have a) good journey*
BOWS, *forward part of a vessel, where it curves to the stem*
BROUGHT UP *(p. 46), halted and anchored the vessel*

'CHANGE, *place such as the Royal Exchange or the Stock Exchange in London, where merchants, financiers and their employees transact business. Thus* MEN ON 'CHANGE, *merchants, businessmen*
CHAPMAN LIGHTHOUSE, *screw-pile lighthouse erected in 1849 on a mudflat off Canvey Island in the Thames*
CIPHER, *code*
COME TO *(p. 3), anchor*
CONFAB, *confabulation, talk*
CUT UP TO THE QUICK *(p. 57; normally 'cut to the quick'), cut to the most sensitive flesh; sharply pained*

DEAL, *coastal town in Kent*
DEPTFORD, *eastern suburb of London, on the south bank of the Thames, once noted for its dockyard established by King Henry VIII*
DRESSING-CASE, *box or case fitted with toilet articles: comb, brushes, etc.*
DRUBBING, *beating*
DU CALME, DU CALME. ADIEU, *[Remain] calm, calm. Goodbye*

EIGHT-INCH GUN, *large naval gun, the barrel's internal diameter being eight inches (20 cm)*

ELDORADO, *the Golden Land sought in vain by the Spanish conquistadores in America. (From* el dorado, *the gilded man or place)*

ERITH, *port and township on the south side of the Thames, three miles north-west of Dartford*

EVOLUTIONS *(p. 82),* manœuvres

FAIRWAY, *navigable part of a river*

FALERNIAN WINE, *fine wine (praised by Roman poets) from the district of Falernus Ager, lying inland from Neapolis (now Napoli or Naples)*

FAMOUS *(p. 13), Splendid (Gallicism, from* fameux*)*

FETISH *(a) object believed to possess supernatural power; (b) object irrationally sought and prized*

FLEET STREET, *busy street of central London, famed as a centre for newspaper-publishing*

FLOAT *(p. 46), blade of a paddle-wheel*

FOOT-WARMER, *perforated metal box (within a wooden frame) containing a pan for live coals*

THE GAULS, *Cisalpine Gaul and Transalpine Gaul. The former was bounded by the Alps and the Apennines, the latter by the Alps, the Mediterranean, the Pyrenees, the Atlantic and the Rhine*

GRAN' BASSAM, *Grand Bassam, a coastal town of Ivory Coast*

GRAVESEND, *town and port on the south side of the Thames, opposite Tilbury Docks, approximately twenty miles east of central London*

GREENWICH, *eastern borough of London, on the south bank of the Thames; former port and location of a palace*

HALTER *(p. 29), rope or strap (sometimes with headgear) for leading a horse*

HARD A-STARBOARD, *as far as possible to the right*

HELM, *wheel*

HOLLAND, *coase linen cloth*

ICHTHYOSAURUS, *prehistoric marine reptile*

INCONTINENTLY, *(a) immediately; (b) impetuously, wildly*

INTERLOPERS, *unauthorised traders; venturers trespassing on a company's monopoly*

LITTLE POPO, *Anecho, a coastal town in Togo*

MARTINI-HENRY, *breech-action rifle, the breech designed by F. Martini and the barrel by A. Henry; the British service rifle between 1876 and 1886*

MEPHISTOPHELES, *a devil who, as Lucifer's agent, is prominent in the Faust legend*

MOTLEY, *multicoloured or particoloured garb, as worn by jesters*

MUFFS *(p. 30; slang), bunglers, incompetent people*

OFFING, *the part of the sea that can be seen from the shore*

OUGH!, *exclamation of distaste or disgust, loosely corresponding to the present-day exclamation 'Yuck!'*

PAPIER-MÂCHÉ, *paper or paper-pulp treated with adhesive and moulded*

PORTICO, *covered entrance to a building, sometimes fronted by columns*

PURCHASES *(p. 45), leverages*

RAVENNA, *town of north-east Italy near the Adriatic coast. The Roman emperor Augustus (63 BC—14 AD) made its port, Classis, into a naval station*

REACH *(p. 51), length of river between bends;* OPENED THE REACH MORE, *proceeded further round the bend into the open stretch*

SCOW, *barge or flat-bottomed vessel*

SECULAR, *age-old, long-lived, ancient*

SHADE *(pp. 59, 84, 94), ghost*

SHAKES, *uncontrollable trembling caused by fever*

SHEERED, *steered on a deviating course*

SHOT DOWN *(p. 36), thrown down, dumped*

SIDE-SPRING BOOTS, *boots with elasticated side-strips*

SIERRA LEONE, *country on the west coast of central Africa. Its capital, Freetown (founded by freed slaves in 1792), was colonised by the British, and the interior became a British protectorate in 1896. Independence was gained in 1961*

SNAG, *hazard to navigation, particularly a submerged or semi-submerged part of a tree*

SOUGHING, *sighing*

SPRIT, *spar set diagonally upwards from the mast, to extend and elevate a fore-and-aft sail (i.e. a sail set lengthwise, rather than sideways across the vessel)*

SQUIRTS *(p. 55; slang), repeating rifles*

STANCHION, *upright supporting-post*

TAMBOV, *city and region of central Russia, about 300 miles south-east of Moscow*

TRIREME, *galley with three banks of oars on each side*

TRUCKLE-BED, *low bed on wheels*

TWILL, *woven fabric showing diagonal lines*

TWO-PENNY-HALFPENNY *(pronounced 'tuppnee-hapenee'), cheap and shoddy*

ULSTER, *long double-breasted overcoat*

VERMUTH, *vermouth, a wine-based drink flavoured with wormwood (absinth)*

WHITE-LEAD, *type of putty made from lead carbonate and linseed oil*

WINCHESTERS, *American repeating-rifles named after O. F. Winchester, their manufacturer; developed around 1866*

WORSTED, *woollen yarn or thread, or fabric made from this*

YAWL, *two-masted sailing vessel, rigged fore-and-aft, with a large mainmast and a small mizzenmast (rear mast)*

CONRAD AND HIS CRITICS

The following selection of material, arranged in chronological order, gives early comments on the tale, followed by some influential tributes, and concludes with further illustrations of the critical controversies mentioned in the Introduction of this volume.

Conrad: letter to Cunninghame Graham, 8 February 1899, in *Joseph Conrad's Letters to R. B. Cunninghame Graham*, ed. C. T. Watts (London: Cambridge University Press, 1969), p. 116.

> I am simply in the seventh heaven, to find you like the *H of D* so far. You bless me indeed. Mind you don't curse me by and bye for the very same thing. There are two more instalments in which the idea is so wrapped up in secondary notions that You – even You! – may miss it. And also you must remember that I don't start with an abstract notion. I start with definite images and as their rendering is true some little effect is produced. So far the note struck chimes in with your convictions – mais après? There is an après. But I think that if you look a little into the episodes you will find in them the right intention though I fear nothing that is practically effective.

Hugh Clifford: 'The Art of Mr. Joseph Conrad': *The Spectator*, 89 (29 November 1902), p. 828:

> 'The Heart of Darkness' . . . . . makes a stronger appeal than anything which its author has yet written . . . . . It is a sombre study of the Congo – the scene is obviously intended to be the Congo, though no names are mentioned – in which, while the inefficiency of certain types of European 'administrators' is mercilessly gibbeted, the power of the wilderness, of contact with barbarism and elemental men and facts, to effect the demoralisation of the white man is conveyed with marvellous force. The denationalisation of the European, the 'going Fantee' of the civilised man, has been treated often enough in fiction . . . . . but never has the 'why of it' been appreciated by any author as Mr. Conrad here appreciates it,

and never, beyond all question, has any writer till now succeeded in bringing the reason, and the ghastly unreason, of it all home to sheltered folk as does Mr. Conrad in this wonderful, this magnificent, this terrible study.

Edward Garnett: review in *Academy and Literature*, 6 December 1902, p. 606:

On reading 'Heart of Darkness' on its appearance in *Blackwood's Magazine* our first impression was that Mr. Conrad had, here and there, lost his way. Now that the story can be read, not in parts, but from the first page to the last at a sitting, we retract this opinion and hold 'Heart of Darkness' to be the high-water mark of the author's talent . . . . . [T]he art of 'Heart of Darkness' implies the catching of infinite shades of the white man's uneasy, disconcerted, and fantastic relations with the exploited barbarism of Africa; it implies the acutest analysis of the deterioration of the white man's *morale*, when he is let loose from European restraint, and planted down in the tropics as an 'emissary of light' armed to the teeth, to make trade profits out of the 'subject races.' The weirdness, the brilliance, the psychological truth of this masterly analysis of two Continents in conflict . . . . . is conveyed in a rapidly rushing narrative which calls for close attention . . . . .

Joseph Conrad: 'Author's Note' [1917] to *Youth* (London: Heinemann, 1921), p. xii:

'Heart of Darkness' is experience . . . . . pushed a little (and only very little) beyond the actual facts of the case for the perfectly legitimate, I believe, purpose of bringing it home to the minds and bosoms of the readers . . . . . That sombre theme had to be given a sinister resonance, a tonality of its own, a continued vibration that, I hoped, would hang in the air and dwell on the ear after the last note had been struck.

F. R. Leavis: *The Great Tradition* (London: Chatto & Windus, 1948), pp. 174, 176, 177, 180:

Heart of Darkness is, by common consent, one of Conrad's best things . . . . . Ordinary greed, stupidity and moral squalor are made to look like behaviour in a lunatic asylum against the vast and oppressive mystery of the surroundings, rendered potently in terms of sensation . . . . . There are, however, places in *Heart of Darkness* where we become aware of comment as an interposition . . . . . Hadn't he, we find ourselves asking, overworked 'inscrutable',

'inconceivable', 'unspeakable' and that kind of word already? . . . . .
He is intent on making a virtue out of not knowing what he means.

Robert F. Haugh: *Joseph Conrad: Discovery in Design* (Norman:
University of Oklahoma Press, 1957), p. 55:

> Conrad's hero may leap high into the rarefied air as does Jim, or
> plunge deep into the darkness of the pit as does Kurtz; in his
> remarkable actions he defines the mortal condition, and in his last
> moment of vision he sees all the scheme of the universe; and we share
> it in a moment of tragic exaltation. But for most of us fidelity to
> household gods is the clue to 'how to be'; our leaky boilers hold us to
> surface truths, even as we learn the meaning of life from the moral
> adventurers who go to their deaths at the far rims of the universe.

Jocelyn Baines: *Joseph Conrad: A Critical Biography* (London:
Weidenfeld & Nicolson, 1960), p. 230:

> In a corrupt world one is bound to commit a corrupt act . . . . .
> [Marlow] had gained his knowledge but lost his innocence.
> It is not, however, this somewhat esoteric meaning that has gained
> 'Heart of Darkness' its exalted position in literature. Conrad's
> achievement consisted primarily in his creation of visual scene upon
> visual scene charged with emotive impact – from the French
> man-of-war shelling the coast, the grove of death, and the journey
> up the river, to the wresting of Kurtz from the wilderness and his
> death on the boat – to attain the cumulative effect of human
> imbecility, of evil and horror.

Lionel Trilling: *Sincerity and Authenticity* [1971] (London: Oxford
University Press, 1972), p. 106:

> What I take to be the paradigmatic literary expression of the modern
> concern with authenticity in Joseph Conrad's great short novel
> *Heart of Darkness*, which appeared, with some appropriateness, in
> the next to the last year of the nineteenth century. This troubling
> work has no manifest polemical intention but it contains in sum the
> whole of the radical critique of European civilization that has been
> made by literature in the years since its publication.

C. B. Cox: Introduction to *Youth: A Narrative / Heart of Darkness / The
End of the Tether* (London: Dent, 1974, rpt 1992), pp. vii, xi–xii:

> This masterpiece ['Heart of Darkness'] has become one of those
> amazing modern fictions, such as Thomas Mann's *Death in Venice*
> or Kafka's *The Trial*, which throw light on the whole nature of
> twentieth-century art, its problems and achievements.

. . . . . Anti-Imperialists emphasize the suffering and torture of the natives. . . . . From the Marxist point of view, Kurtz is seen as an embodiment of all the evils which are produced by free enterprise in a capitalist system. In complete contrast, some readers find in Kurtz a devil whose fascinations, like those of Milton's Satan, it may be difficult to resist. The Jungians discover in the story a night journey into the unconscious . . . . . The adventure down the Congo has also been analysed as a Freudian voyage into the wilderness of sex . . . . .

There is no one key which will unlock the secret meaning of 'Heart of Darkness'.

Chinua Achebe: 'An Image of Africa' [1975]: *The Massachusetts Review*, 18 (1977), pp. 788–9:

Conrad was a bloody racist . . . . . A Conrad student told me in Scotland last year that Africa is merely the setting for the disintegration of the mind of Mr. Kurtz.

Which is partly the point: Africa as setting and backdrop which eliminates the African as human factor. Africa as a metaphysical battlefield devoid of all recognizable humanity, into which the wandering European enters at his peril . . . . . All those men in Nazi Germany who lent their talent to the service of virulent racism whether in science, philosophy or the arts have generally and rightly been condemned for their perversions. The time is long overdue for taking a hard look at the work of creative artists who apply their talents, alas often considerable as in the case of Conrad, to set people against people.

Terry Eagleton: *Criticism and Ideology* [1976] (London: Verso, 1978), pp. 137, 140:

Work for Conrad is a self-sacrificial sharing in the social totality, but like Kurtz's labours in *Heart of Darkness* merely exposes one's estrangement from the eternally elusive Nature which is to be reduced to order. Aesthetic form must vanquish the inchoate, as imperialism strives to subdue the 'disorganisation' of tribal society to rational order; yet such ordering always contains its own negation . . . . . The need for value, and the recognition of its utter vacuity: it is here that the deepest contradiction of Conrad's enterprise, one integral to the imperialist ideology he shared, stands revealed.

Frances B. Singh: 'The Colonialist Bias of *Heart of Darkness*': *Conradiana*, 10 (1978), pp. 44, 52, 53:

Historically Marlow would have us feel that the Africans are the innocent victims of the white man's heart of darkness; psychologically and metaphysically he would have us believe that they have the power to turn the white man's heart black . . . . . I do not wish to suggest that Conrad intended *Heart of Darkness* as a vindication of colonialistic policies or that the story should be removed from the canon of works indicting colonialism . . . . . Nevertheless for the modern reader his limitations reduce the significance of his achievement as a psychologist and a moralist, ironically turning a story that was meant to be a clear-cut attack on a vicious system into a partial apology for it, and a study of the depths in all men into an excuse for their existence.

C. P. Sarvan: 'Racism and the *Heart of Darkness*': *The International Fiction Review*, 7 (1980), pp. 9, 10:

Achebe . . . . . noted that Kurtz's African mistress is the 'savage counterpart to the refined, European woman' . . . . . But the European woman is pale and rather anemic whilst the former, to use Conrad's words, is gorgeous, proud, superb, magnificent, tragic, fierce, and filled with sorrow . . . . . She is an impressive figure and, importantly, her human feelings are not denied . . . . .

In a conversation with me, Ngugi Wa Thiong'o accepted some of Achebe's criticisms but felt he had overlooked the positive aspect, namely, Conrad's attack on colonialism. The skulls stuck on poles outside Kurtz's house, Wa Thiong'o said, was the most powerful indictment of colonialism . . . . . But Wa Thiong'o also observed that though Conrad (having experienced the evils of Czarist imperialism) castigates Belgian atrocities, he is much milder in his criticisms of British imperialism . . . . . Conrad . . . . . was not entirely immune to the infection of the beliefs and attitudes of his age, but he was ahead of most in trying to break free.

Wilson Harris: 'The Frontier on Which *Heart of Darkness* Stands': *Research in African Literatures*, 12 (1981), pp. 86, 88:

Achebe's essay . . . . . is . . . . . a persuasive argument, but I am convinced his judgement or dismissal of *Heart of Darkness* – and of Conrad's strange genius – is a profoundly mistaken one. He sees the distortions of imagery and, therefore, of character in the novel as witnessing to horrendous prejudice . . . . .

The most significant distortion of imagery in *Heart of Darkness* bears upon Kurtz's liberal manifesto of imperial good and moral light. In that manifesto or consolidation of virtues the 'extermination of aii the [alien] brutes' becomes inevitable. Thus Conrad parodies the notion of moral light that devours all in its path – a parody that cuts to the heart of paternalism with strings attached to each filial puppet.

Hunt Hawkins: 'Joseph Conrad, Roger Casement, and the Congo Reform Movement': *Journal of Modern Literature*, 9 (1981), p. 80:

[T]he Congo Reform Association . . . . settled on the pragmatic solution of removing the Congo from Leopold's personal control and giving it to Belgium to be administered by the Belgian parliament. After an intense international campaign . . . . , this goal was finally achieved on 15 November 1908. While the 'Belgian solution' was far from perfect, it at least ended the very worst excesses of Leopold's regime, including alienation of communal African land and forced labor.

. . . . . Conrad was overly pessimistic when he told Cunninghame Graham that *Heart of Darkness* contained 'the right intention though I fear nothing that is practically effective.' We cannot know how many people Conrad's Congo fiction informed and moved to indignation, but we at least know that, despite its overshadowing darkness, Conrad's work provided solid inspiration to the reformers. On 7 October 1909, after the campaign against Leopold had proven successful, E. D. Morel gave Conrad the highest praise when he said in a letter to A. Conan Doyle that *Heart of Darkness* was the 'most powerful thing ever written on the subject.'

Nina Pelikan Straus: 'The Exclusion of the Intended from Secret Sharing in Conrad's *Heart of Darkness*': *Novel*, 20 (1987), p. 135:

Because the female figure's psychic penury is so valuable in asserting the heroism of the Strong Poet and the Strong Poet's character, the male commentator (who serves both) is filled with pleasure . . . . .

Because the woman reader is not so 'filled,' she is in the position to insist that Marlow's cowardice consists of his inability to face the dangerous self that is the form of his own masculinist vulnerability: his own complicity in the racist, sexist, imperialist, and finally libidinally satisfying world he has inhabited with Kurtz . . . . .

Does *Heart of Darkness* become less authentic, less finally recognizable as the truth of our times, when it is recognized that it is less the comprehensive human Id that is disclosed than a certain kind of male self-mystification whose time is passing if not past?

Bette London: *The Appropriated Voice: Narrative Authority in Conrad, Forster, and Woolf* (Ann Arbor: University of Michigan Press, 1990), pp. 44, 45, 49:

Marlow virulently discredits the world of women, while the life of

the natives remains beyond his conceptual reach . . . . . Bound to
Kurtz, Marlow doubles for the prospective bride; he usurps her
place as Kurtz's chosen . . . . . Marlow's reconstruction of the
domain of masculinity positions his audience in woman's place:
excluded from knowledge, truth, and adventure – excluded from
even imginative entry into man's terrain. In the scenario Marlow
articulates, his audience inhabits the familiar realm of domesticity,
coded as feminine . . . . .

SUGGESTIONS FOR FURTHER READING

Biographies of Conrad:

Jocelyn Baines: *Joseph Conrad: A Critical Biography* (London: Weidenfeld & Nicolson, 1960; Harmondsworth: Penguin, 1971). Lucid, concise and useful, though now out-of-date in some respects.
Frederick R. Karl: *Joseph Conrad: The Three Lives* (New York: Farrar, Straus and Giroux, 1979). Big, resourceful, speculative.
Zdzisław Najder: *Joseph Conrad: A Chronicle* (Cambridge: Cambridge University Press, 1983). A scholarly, well-documented study.
John Batchelor: *The Life of Joseph Conrad* (Oxford: Blackwell, 1994). Concise, with numerous lively details.

Anthologies containing reviews and critical essays:

Conrad: The Critical Heritage, ed. Norman Sherry (London and Boston: Routledge & Kegan Paul, 1973).
Joseph Conrad: Critical Assessments (4 volumes), ed. Keith Carabine (Robertsbridge: Helm Information, 1992).

Critical and scholarly books which discuss 'Heart of Darkness':

F. R. Leavis: *The Great Tradition* (London: Chatto & Windus, 1948; Harmondsworth: Penguin, 1962). Contains a very influential discussion of Conrad.
Robert F. Haugh: *Joseph Conrad: Discovery in Design* (Norman: University of Oklahoma Press, 1957). Emphasises the importance of such 'moral adventurers' as Kurtz.
Albert Guerard: *Conrad the Novelist* (Cambridge, Mass.: Harvard University Press, 1958; New York: Athenaeum, 1967). Jungian, imaginative and suggestive; particularly helpful in its specifications of Conradian paradoxes.

Conrad's 'Heart of Darkness' and the Critics, ed. Bruce Harkness (Belmont: Wadsworth, 1960). An early 'case-book', now rather out-of-date.

Heart of Darkness: Backgrounds and Criticism, ed. L. F. Dean (Englewood Cliffs, N.J.: Prentice-Hall, 1960). Another early case-book.

E. K. Hay: *The Political Novels of Joseph Conrad* (Chicago and London: Chicago University Press, 1963; 2nd edn, 1981). Emphasises the humanely liberal aspects of Conrad's outlook.

Joseph Conrad: *Heart of Darkness*, ed. Robert Kimbrough (New York and London: Norton, 1963, 1971, 1988). The most comprehensive and influential of the case-books.

Norman Sherry: *Conrad's Western World* (London: Cambridge University Press, 1971). Shrewd detective-work on the factual sources of 'Heart of Darkness'.

Lionel Trilling: *Sincerity and Authenticity* (Harvard: Harvard University Press, 1971; London: Oxford University Press, 1972). Stressed the cultural centrality of Conrad's tale.

Terry Eagleton: *Criticism and Ideology* (London: New Left Books, 1976; London: Verso, 1978). Includes a brilliantly innovatory, succinct and challenging account of Conrad's political plight.

Cedric Watts: *Conrad's 'Heart of Darkness': A Critical and Contextual Discussion* (Milano: Mursia International, 1977). Approaches the tale from numerous angles.

Ian Watt: *Conrad in the Nineteenth Century* (Berkeley: California University Press, 1979; London: Chatto & Windus, 1980). Provides an impressively full, sophisticated and urbane analysis of 'Heart of Darkness' and its cultural milieu.

Cedric Watts: *A Preface to Conrad* (London and New York: Longman, 1982; 2nd edn, 1993). A concise introduction to Conrad's works.

Joseph Conrad's 'Heart of Darkness', ed. Harold Bloom (New York and Philadelphia: Chelsea House, 1987). A selection of items by critics from the 1950s onwards.

Literary Theory at Work: Three Texts, ed. Douglas Tallack (London: Batsford; Totowa, N, J.: Barnes and Noble; 1987). Includes Diana Knight on narratology, David Murray on 'dialogics' and Steve Smith on Marxism and ideology.

Jetty van de Vriesenaerde: *Conrad Criticism 1965–1985: Heart of Darkness* (Groningen: Phoenix Press, 1988). Summaries and critical appraisals of a broad selection of commentaries.

Joseph Conrad: 'Heart of Darkness': A Case Study in Contemporary

Criticism, ed. Ross C. Murfin (New York: St Martin's Press, 1989). The approaches purport to be variously psychoanalytic, 'reader-response', feminist, deconstructive and 'new historicist'.

Anthony Fothergill: *Heart of Darkness* (Milton Keynes and Philadelphia: Open University Press, 1989). Congenially clear in its use of the question-and-discussion format.

Marianna Torgovnick: *Gone Primitive: Savage Intellects, Modern Lives* (Chicago and London: University of Chicago Press, 1990). Stresses literary interlinkages of the female with the primitive.

Bette London: *The Appropriated Voice: Narrative Authority in Conrad, Forster, and Woolf* (Ann Arbor: Michigan University Press, 1990). A vigorous feminist argument.

Richard Adams: *Joseph Conrad: 'Heart of Darkness'* (London: Penguin, 1991). A proficient introductory discussion of the tale.

Robert Burden: *Heart of Darkness* (Basingstoke and London: Macmillan, 1991). 'This book . . . . . is as much about critical theory as it is about HD': sophisticated, widely-ranging, concise.

Ruth L. Nadelhaft: *Joseph Conrad* (Hemel Hempstead: Harvester Wheatsheaf, 1991). Argues that Conrad depicts women as centres of resistance to male vanity and imperialist assumptions.

Daphna Erdinast-Vulcan: *Joseph Conrad and the Modern Temper* (Oxford: Oxford University Press, 1991). Sees Conrad as 'an incurable moralist infected with the ethical relativism of his age'.

Andrea White: *Joseph Conrad and the Adventure Tradition* (Cambridge: Cambridge University Press, 1993). Shows how Conrad adopts and adapts the materials of narratives of adventure.

Critical and scholarly essays on 'Heart of Darkness':

Chinua Achebe: 'An Image of Africa': *The Chancellor's Lecture Series: 1974–75* (Amherst: University of Massachusetts, 1975), reprinted in *Massachusetts Review*, 18 (1977), pp. 782–94, and in *Research in African Literatures*, 9 (1978), pp. 1–15. A revised version appears in Achebe's *Hopes and Impediments* (London: Heinemann, 1988; New York: Doubleday, 1989), pp. 1–20, and in the volumes edited by Carabine and Kimbrough, cited above. In either version, a radically challenging piece.

Tzvetan Todorov: 'Knowledge in the Void: *Heart of Darkness*' [1975]: *Conradiana*, 21 (1989), pp. 161–72. Suggests that the tale, like Kurtz, is 'hollow at the core'.

Frances B. Singh: 'The Colonialistic Bias of Heart of Darkness':
Conradiana, 10 (1978), pp. 41–54. Reprinted in Kimbrough, pp. 268–
80. Qualifies Achebe's argument.

Hunt Hawkins: 'Conrad's Critique of Imperialism in Heart of Darkness':
P.M.L.A. [Publications of the Modern Language Association of
America], 94 (January 1979), pp. 286–99. A well-researched discussion.

C. P. Sarvan: 'Racism and the Heart of Darkness': International Fiction
Review, 7 (1980), pp. 6–10. Reprinted in Kimbrough, pp. 280–5. Like
Singh and Harris, Sarvan extends the debate initiated by Achebe.

Wilson Harris: 'The Frontier on Which Heart of Darkness Stands':
Research in African Literatures, 12 (1981). pp. 86–93. Reprinted in
Kimbrough, pp. 262–8.

Hunt Hawkins: 'Joseph Conrad, Roger Casement, and the Congo
Reform Movement': Journal of Modern Literature, 9 (1981), pp. 65–80.
Clear, scholarly and informative.

Hunt Hawkins: 'The Issue of Racism in Heart of Darkness': Conradiana,
14 (1982), pp. 163–71. Balanced and scrupulous.

Peter Nazareth: 'Out of Darkness: Conrad and Other Third World
Writers': Conradiana, 14 (1982), pp. 173–87. A usefully concise survey.

Cedric Watts: ' "A Bloody Racist": About Achebe's View of Conrad':
Yearbook of English Studies, 13 (1983), pp. 196–209. Reprinted in
Carabine, Vol. 2, pp. 405–18. A defence of Conrad and 'Heart of
Darkness'.

Nina Pelikan Straus: 'The Exclusion of the Intended from Secret Sharing
in Conrad's Heart of Darkness': Novel, 20 (1987), pp. 123–37.
Reprinted in Carabine, Vol. 2, pp. 349–63. Sees Marlow as a deplorable
male chauvinist.

Daniel R. Schwarz: 'Teaching Heart of Darkness: Towards a Pluralistic
Perspective': Conradiana, 24 (1992), pp. 191–206. Closely relates the
practice of teaching to the interpretation of 'Heart of Darkness'.

TEXT SUMMARY

Part I

Preamble:

On the yawl *Nellie*, anchored on the Thames, five friends await the turn of the tide; one of them considers the river's history. Another, Charles Marlow, after reflecting on ancient Roman and subsequent modes of imperialism, commences a narrative of his journey into central Africa.

Marlow's narrative:

Thanks to the influence of his aunt, Marlow gains employment with a Continental company which organises trading in the region of the Congo. He voyages to Africa in a French steamer, then travels up-river to the Company's outer station. The Europeans' activities there seem to be chaotic, rapacious and cruel: Marlow sees some Africans toiling in a chain-gang, while others are dying of disease and starvation. He hears about the remarkable Mr Kurtz, a successful and apparently idealistic ivory-trader who works at a remote outpost. Marlow then treks overland to the central station, where he finds that the steamboat which he expected to command has been mysteriously wrecked. The repairs take months, during which Marlow (repelled by the incompetence and greed of the European traders) learns that the manager sees Kurtz as a rival for promotion.

Part II

Marlow's narrative continues:

A conversation between the manager and his uncle reveals the manager's hope that Kurtz will die in the wilderness. Eventually the steamboat is repaired and heads upstream, commanded by Marlow, with the manager, various ivory-hunting 'pilgrims' and the cannibal crew aboard. The journey takes them through dense jungle whose inhabitants are glimpsed from time to time: an environment which Marlow finds variously oppressive, disturbing and enigmatic. At a mooring-place he finds a manual of seamanship and a note of warning. Later, after being impeded by fog, the steamboat is attacked; Marlow's helmsman is killed by a thrown spear.

At the inner station, Kurtz is dying, and is apparently deranged. His eloquent report for the 'International Society for the Suppression of Savage Customs' ends with the words: 'Exterminate all the brutes!'

Part III

Marlow's narrative continues:

From observation and from conversations with a young Russian adventurer, Marlow learns that Kurtz had become a worshipped chieftain, a participant in diabolical rites; revered by the local Africans, he had led them on pillaging expeditions: 'his soul was mad'. Though close to death, Kurtz now makes an attempt to return to a ritual in the jungle, where a horned and 'fiend-like' figure apparently presides; but Marlow heads him off and brings him back to the vessel.

As the steamboat prepares to leave, the Africans gather on the bank, the central personage being the imposing woman who was Kurtz's consort. The 'pilgrims' open fire; Marlow scatters the crowd by sounding the steam-whistle. Kurtz discourses at length during the voyage downstream, revealing his megalomania and confusion; his last words are, 'The horror! The horror!' – a victory of sorts. He dies and is buried in a muddy hole.

In the European city, Marlow, who has been afflicted with feverish illness, takes a jaded view of the crowds around him. He decides to visit Kurtz's fiancée, however, because her picture had seemed beautiful. At their meeting, Marlow lies in order to preserve the fiancée's idealistic faith in Kurtz.

Here Marlow ends his narrative. The yawl *Nellie* is encompassed by night, and the Thames seems to lead 'into the heart of an immense darkness'.

ACKNOWLEDGEMENTS

The editor is grateful to Hans van Marle (for generous and detailed advice), Brian Nicholas (for information on Gallicisms), Alan Sinfield (for encouragement and help with the proofs), and the staff of the Inter-Library Loans Department at Sussex University Library.

The editor and publishers wish to thank the following for permission to use copyright material:

Conradiana for material from Frances B. Singh, 'The Colonialist Bias of *Heart of Darkness*', *Conradiana*, 10, 1978, pp. 44, 52, 53;

The Massachusetts Review for material from Chinua Achebe, 'An Image of Africa', *The Massachusetts Review*, 18, 1977, pp. 788–9. Copyright © 1977 The Massachusetts Review;

Oxford University Press for material from Lionel Trilling, *Sincerity and Authenticity*, 1972;

Random Century UK Ltd and New York University Press for material from F. R. Leavis, *The Great Tradition*, Chatto & Windus, 1948, pp. 174, 176–7, 180;

University of Michigan Press for material from Bette London, The *Appropriated Voice: Narrative Authority in Conrad, Forster, and Woolf*, pp. 44, 45, 49;

Verso/New Left Books for material from Terry Eagleton, *Criticism and Ideology*, 1976, pp. 137, 140;

Weidenfeld & Nicolson for material from Jocelyn Baines, *Joseph Conrad: A Critical Biography*, 1960.

Every effort has been made to trace all the copyright holders but if any have been inadvertently overlooked the publishers will be pleased to make the necessary arrangement at the first opportunity.